DEATH SHALL COME

A Selection of Recent Titles by Simon R. Green

* available from Severn House

DEATH SHALL COME

An Ishmael Jones mystery

Simon R. Green

Severn House Large Print
London & New York

This first large print edition published 2018
in Great Britain and the USA by
SEVERN HOUSE PUBLISHERS LTD of
Eardley House, 4 Uxbridge Street, London W8 7SY.
First world regular print edition published 2017 by
Severn House Publishers Ltd.

British Library Cataloguing in Publication Data
A CIP catalogue record for this title is available from the British Library.

ISBN-13: 9780727893505

Severn House Publishers support the Forest Stewardship Council™
[FSC™], the leading international forest certification organisation. All
our titles that are printed on FSC certified paper carry the FSC logo.

Typeset by Palimpsest Book Production Ltd.,
Falkirk, Stirlingshire, Scotland.
Printed and bound in Great Britain by
T J International, Padstow, Cornwall.

Call me Ishmael. Ishmael Jones.

I go walking in dangerous places, and if I do my job right no one ever knows I'm there. I work for an organization that doesn't officially exist, dealing with all the weird and unnatural things that shouldn't exist in any sane and rational world. It's my job to deal with what lurks in the shadows, on the borders of the rational, and stamp on them hard if they look like getting out of hand. To keep Humanity safe, and blissfully unaware of just how big the world really is.

Back in 1963 a star fell from the heavens to land in an English field. Or, to put it another way, an alien starship dropped screaming from the outer dark and buried itself in the earth. Before I left the cracked-open ship its trans-formation machines made me human, right down to my DNA, so I could walk the Earth unobserved. But the machines were damaged in the crash, and they wiped all my previous memories.

Of who and what I used to be.

I haven't aged a day since I first came to myself, staggering bewildered across a forgotten field, in 1963. I like to think of myself as human.

1

It's all I ever want to be. But sometimes in my dreams I look into my mirror and catch glimpses of something else looking back at me . . . Then I wake up screaming.

Together with my partner and my love, Penny Belcourt, I solve mysteries and protect people from all the monsters of the hidden world. And sometimes from the monsters inside people.

I walk among you, but I'm not one of you. Which is probably why I'm so good at seeing things and people for what they really are.

One
In the Midst of Death

Death shall come on swift wings to whoever desecrates this tomb. An ancient curse, supposedly unleashed on the archaeologists who broke into the tomb of Tutankhamun. A number of people connected to the tomb's desecration died suddenly, mysteriously and sometimes horribly. Even those who left Egypt to return home. Whatever it was that flew on swift wings, it pursued its prey wherever they fled.

Of course, that all happened a long time ago. No one believes in such superstitions these days.

When you don't officially exist, you can't afford to stand out. I live in small hotels, boarding houses and rented rooms, always moving on before anyone can notice me. These days, with so many cameras everywhere, I'm not even safe walking down the street. So I just keep moving from place to place, using this name and that, always dealing strictly in cash, while I wait for the Organization to call and put me to work again. There are lots of people like me; not so much homeless as rootless. Living very private lives off the grid and under the radar, for any number of perfectly good reasons. Hiding from the people who would hurt us, if they could. Denied the

3

comforts of close friends or families, or any of the ties that bind. Because we're different.

And yet, knowing all this, I still fell in love. After all, I'm only human. And that's when my life got really complicated. Because one of the main definitions of love is when someone else's safety and happiness becomes more important than your own. My love, my fellow conspirator and partner in crimes: my Penny Belcourt. I can't live with her, or plan for a future together; but I share as much of my life with her as I can.

Sometimes I think I've never been happier, and sometimes I think I've never been more scared. That something will happen to her, as well as me.

My latest case started with a visit to the Ancient Egypt rooms at the British Museum. I'd been summoned to this venerable institution by the Colonel, my only personal contact with the Organization. After all the years I've worked for them, doing good work for the good of my soul, I still have no idea who or what they really are. It's enough that we have interests in common, and look out for each other as well as the world. So when the Colonel calls, on the very private number that only he knows, I always answer. Because that was the deal I made with the Organization: service in return for protection.

Museums make for excellent meeting places. Always lots of crowds to hide in, and a multitude of interesting things to draw attention away from me. I made a point of casually strolling into the museum lobby at midday, when it was sure to be packed with holiday crowds and noisy packs of schoolchildren. My clothes were nicely anonymous, and I kept the peak of my baseball cap pulled well down to hide my face in shadow from the ever-present cameras. The cap bore a logo from the film *Alien*, because you have to find your laughs where you can. I eased through the bustling crowds like a ghost, quiet and remote; and no one knew I was there.

Even the uniformed security guards paid me no attention, because I have learned to move in public without being noticed. To be just another face in the crowd, of no interest to anyone. It's all in the walk and the body language. Security cameras are another matter: those unblinking observers of every moment and every person. Society's merciless conscience. The Organization is supposed to make sure I never show up on any recordings; but I haven't survived this long by relying on the efficiency of strangers. I put more faith in my baseball cap.

I wandered around for a while, just to make sure no one was lying in wait for me, and then casually made my way to the upper floor, heading for the burial exhibits in the Egyptian rooms. Taking my time, because something about this particular summons bothered me. The Colonel had been very insistent I come alone, without Penny. He knew we work together these days . . . So what could the Colonel have to say that he didn't want Penny to hear? And what did he think he could say that would stop me telling her everything afterwards?

I was still considering the implications of this

5

as I approached rooms 62 and 63. Then I suddenly realized that the crowds had faded away and I was on my own. I stopped at the entrance and looked around thoughtfully. The rooms hadn't been officially closed off with NO ENTRY signs or apologetic little notices about cleaning or safety or refurbishment. But the word had clearly gone out, and museum people had been put in place to steer the general public away. When the Organization speaks, everyone listens. Even if they're not sure why. And yet no one had tried to stop me – which suggested that not only was I expected but someone had told them who to look for. I really didn't like that.

I seriously considered turning around and heading for the exit with all speed. But the Colonel had called . . . and I was curious. As I stepped cautiously into the Egyptian rooms, the first thing I noticed was that all the surveillance systems had been turned off. Not a movement or a winking light anywhere. Whatever the Colonel and I were here to talk about, no one was going to know but us.

I strolled through the exhibits, ostentatiously calm and relaxed. Taking in the coffins and the mummies, the funerary masks and stylized portraits . . . and all the other things the Ancient Egyptians had meant to stay buried with their honoured dead. Some of the exhibits were protected inside glass cases, while others were set out on pedestals; but most had just been laid out quite casually, under helpful explanatory signs, on long tables. The bric-à-brac of ages, everyday items made special and significant just

6

by the passing of time. Pots and pans and household junk, most of which had probably looked seriously ugly even in their day. Lots of gold, and lots of things with enigmatic cat faces. The Ancient Egyptians liked gold, and cats. There was no sign of the Colonel anywhere.

The air was heavy with all kinds of scents. Spices, preservatives, dust and cleaning products. For me, the world is saturated with odours packed with information. I've learned to tune most of them out, in self-defence.

I don't know how dogs stand it. But then, they sniff each other's arses. Because they want to.

The museum likes to call this particular collection a celebration of eternal life, but really it's like walking through a graveyard with its own concession stands. All the trappings and accessories of the ancient funeral trade; to help you contemplate your own mortality, and ram home the point that you really can't take it with you. Because even if you try, someone will only dig it up and put it in a museum. Don't let the scholars fool you, it's nothing to do with accumulating treasures from the past. It's all about trophies. To show who's in charge, and who's ahead in the game.

I have thought about my own death. I was made human from something else and, while I'm pretty sure I could be killed by any number of things, I haven't aged a day in more than fifty years. Perhaps one day, thousands of years from now, I'll visit another museum and walk among exhibits from this culture, from this time. I wonder how I'll feel about them then.

I finally ended up before a standing sarcophagus. No glass case, no protections, even though it was covered with gold. The dully burnished metal gleamed sullenly under the bright lights as if it resented the attention. And although the lid was still in place, it was entirely blank. None of the usual exquisite detailing or stylized artwork. No face, no name; an entirely anonymous death. The Unknown Mummy. I considered my distorted reflection in the gleaming surface; almost human, but not quite. I looked round sharply as I heard footsteps approaching. And there was the Colonel, striding briskly through the exhibits with his usual stiff-backed military bearing.

He had dressed for this meeting in what he obviously considered to be unremarkable clothes, so he wouldn't stand out. Instead of the usual impeccably tailored Savile Row three-piece suit, he'd settled for a dark blazer over grey slacks. But he was still wearing his old-school tie and there was no disguising his ex-military background, where arrogance comes as standard. The Colonel didn't know how to look like anything but officer material. A tall striking presence in his late thirties, he was handsome enough in a supercilious kind of way; right down to the neatly trimmed military moustache. He nodded briefly as he crashed to a halt in front of me and tried for a cordial smile, but couldn't quite bring it off.

I nodded easily back at him, stuck my hands in my pockets, and slouched. Just because I knew that would irritate him. First rule in dealing with authority figures: never give them an inch or they'll walk all over you. My interest was piqued as I realized there was something different about the Colonel's body language. Normally the man was so stiff and formal I half expected him to pull a muscle from sheer internal discipline. But today the Colonel looked . . . troubled. My first thought was that he was nervous because he'd brought me here to lure me into a trap. I looked around quickly, checking the distance to the exit and readying myself for a fight. The Colonel managed his first real smile.

'Relax, Mister Jones. You're in no danger. Not everything is about you. I'm just . . . concerned that what is about to pass between us stays between us. The Organization doesn't know that you and I are meeting here.'

I looked at him thoughtfully. 'That isn't normal procedure.'

'This isn't a normal case,' said the Colonel. 'Though the matter we're about to discuss does have . . . Organization connections.'

He paused, considering his next words carefully. It amused me, to see the normally confident and assured Colonel so off balance.

'All right,' I said. 'I'm intrigued. What's this all about?'

He squared his shoulders and met my gaze steadily, bracing himself to move into territory beyond his normal comfort zone.

'I need you to work on a case outside the Organization. No contact, no backup, no reports. Taking it on would not be part of your usual agreement, it would be more in the nature of a personal favour to me.'

I could see how embarrassed he was to be asking me this, even desperate. My first instinct was to say no and run like hell; but I could tell that something about this case really mattered to the Colonel.

'Are you in trouble?' I said.

'Not me,' said the Colonel. 'But someone close to me might be. Someone I am determined to protect at all costs. I need your help to determine what's really going on. And what to do about it.'

'You want me to run a case without the Organization's knowledge or protection, knowing that if they find out they might cut me loose? You want me to put my hard-earned security at risk, just to help you?'

'Yes,' said the Colonel.

'Why on earth would I do that?'

'I can't think of one good reason,' the Colonel said steadily. 'There's nothing in it for you. But I need this. So I'm asking you, because there's no one else I trust.'

'All right,' I said. 'I'm in. But . . . you will owe me a serious favour in return.'

The Colonel nodded stiffly. 'Understood.'

'Why bring me here to discuss this?' I said. 'Why the Egyptian rooms, in particular?'

'Because it's relevant to the case,' said the Colonel. He was back in control, now I was just hired help again. And he always liked it when he could lecture me about things he knew that I didn't. 'The Cardavan family have been collecting Ancient Egyptian relics and curios for generations, and have assembled a private collection that would be the envy of many major museums

10

if anyone outside the Cardavans' small circle of private collectors ever found out what was in it.'

'You couldn't build a private collection that size through official channels,' I said. 'So we're talking theft, smuggling and bribery on a really impressive scale. How did the Cardavans pull that off?'

'Influence,' said the Colonel. 'They're a very old established family with all kinds of political connections, and until recently almost indecently wealthy. An unbeatable combination when it comes to looting the treasures of other nations. And now the family have acquired their first mummy. George Cardavan paid a great deal of money to get his hands on a famous name from the past that has never seen the inside of any museum. Shipped directly to Cardavan House from its recently discovered tomb in the Valley of the Sorcerers, this mummy is supposed to be the very first Cleopatra . . . A previously unknown progenitor of that famous line, dating back further than the second century BC.'

He paused a moment to make sure I was properly impressed. I felt obliged to make it clear I wasn't entirely ignorant on the subject.

'Most people think there was only the one Cleopatra,' I said. 'Immortalized in legend, and any number of dubious movies. In fact, Mark Antony's Cleopatra was the seventh to bear that name and the last. The last real Pharaoh before Egypt became just another outpost ruled by Rome.' I looked thoughtfully at the Colonel. 'If a previously unknown Cleopatra has turned up, I would have expected it to be all over the news. And I haven't heard anything.'

'And you won't,' said the Colonel. 'No one has and no one will, outside the Cardavan circle. Money talks, and enough of it ensures silence.'

'Except among people like us,' I said.

He smiled briefly. 'It's our job to know the things that matter.'

'How does this matter to the Organization?' I said.

The Colonel looked away for a moment, glancing round the Egyptian rooms, as he made up his mind about how much to tell me. When he finally spoke, he almost seemed to be addressing the exhibits rather than me.

'George Cardavan runs a private security firm attached to Black Heir.'

I nodded slowly. Black Heir is responsible for cleaning up after alien incursions. Hiding the truth, destroying evidence, and quietly gathering up any alien tech left behind. And then just as quietly selling it on the black market to those with an interest in reverse-engineering such things.

I know that, because I used to work for them. Until we came to a sudden parting of the ways, when I found it necessary to disappear in a hurry because someone got the idea I might not be who or even necessarily what I claimed to be. Staying one step ahead of such people is what keeps me alive.

'Cardavan's firm provides warm bodies on the ground,' said the Colonel, meeting my gaze squarely again. 'Trained security personnel, to keep the public at a distance while Black Heir does its job.'

'And make it all officially "Never Happened",' I said. 'Nothing to see here, move along.'

'Quite,' said the Colonel. 'Cardavan's people stand in as police officers, regular army, private security guards. Whatever seems most plausible.'

'Do they also perhaps provide strong-arm tactics on occasion?' I said. 'To lean on a journalist or intimidate a witness?'

'It's that kind of job, sometimes,' said the Colonel. 'Because sometimes it's that kind of world.'

'Men In Black . . .'

'Are nothing more than urban legends,' the Colonel said firmly. 'If I might be allowed to continue . . .'

'Don't let me stop you.'

'George Cardavan's firm has a reputation for doing good, reliable work. Which means the Organization considers him a valuable asset.'

'Are you saying he's untouchable?'

'No,' said the Colonel. 'Just that he's not someone you want to accuse without good cause.'

'Why are you taking such an interest in all this?' I said.

'Because even a man as successful as George Cardavan shouldn't have been able to put up the kind of money it would take to buy a mummy this important,' said the Colonel. 'This goes well beyond bribing a few customs officials to look the other way. To smuggle a find this important out of Egypt and into Britain would take serious corruption in really high places. George might be successful these days, but not that successful. And his family haven't had that kind of money in years. So how was he able to afford it? I have to wonder if he might be selling off Black Heir's secrets – the location of alien crash sites, or what happened to the bodies. He might even be making private deals over alien technology. And some of the people involved in that can be very bad people.'

'Is there any solid evidence to prove he's been selling secrets, or tech?'

'No,' said the Colonel. 'Nothing. That's why I'm bringing you in. To get to the truth.'

'Why are you so determined to keep this off the books?' I said. 'This sounds like a perfectly straight forward Organization case.'

'Because I am married to George Cardavan's daughter,' said the Colonel.

I nodded, as much became clear. 'Are you afraid some of the scandal might rub off on you?'

'No,' said the Colonel. 'My only fear is how it might affect my wife, Chloe. I can't risk an official investigation until I'm sure of what's happening. It's always possible none of this has anything to do with selling secrets or tech. In which case, the Organization doesn't need to know.'

'But why come to me for help?' I said. 'Out of all the Organization agents you run? I haven't worked for Black Heir in years. And it's not as if you and I are friends or anything.'

'Because I know I can rely on you to get to the truth of the matter,' said the Colonel. 'And because I know you know how to keep a secret.'

I met his gaze steadily, but he had nothing more to say.

'What if this does turn out to be something the Organization needs to know about?' I said.

14

'Then you and I will be right there on the spot and on the case, ready to do whatever needs doing.'

'Regardless of how it affects the Cardavans?'

'I know my duty,' said the Colonel. 'Well, now that you know as much as I do, are you still willing to take the case?'

'Of course,' I said. 'I already said yes.'

The Colonel blinked a few times. 'Just like that? No demands or conditions?'

'Just that you'll owe me one.'

'Acceptable,' said the Colonel. I thought for a moment he might smile or offer to shake hands, but he was immediately all business again. 'There is to be a gathering of the family this weekend at Cardavan House. So George can show off his new acquisition to the only people he can trust to stay quiet about it. His immediate family.'

'How many will be present?' I said. 'Anyone I need to know about?'

'Just half a dozen or so. And no names you'd recognize. I will be there, of course, as Chloe's husband. None of them know I work for the Organization.'

'Not even your wife?' I said.

'What she doesn't know can't hurt her,' said the Colonel. 'She knows I used to work for Black Heir, because she still does. But as far as the Cardavans are concerned, I work for some suitably boring Government department.'

I nodded slowly. 'What's my cover story?'

'You will be attending the grand unveiling as my personal expert, there to give your unbiased

15

opinion on the authenticity of the mummy. I've made no secret of my doubts on the matter.'

'I don't know anything about authenticating mummies!'

'Then you'd better read up on the subject,' said the Colonel. 'Enough to sound like you know what you're talking about, and buy the two of us time to discover what lies at the bottom of all this.'

'We've never worked together before,' I said.

'And we won't be, this time. Officially, that is. I shall talk to everyone in a suitably roundabout manner and sound them out on what they know. And while I'm keeping them all occupied, you will burgle George's office. Break into his safe, search his desk, study his records. I need hard evidence before I can take any action.'

'What if I get caught?'

'Then I shall of course disavow all knowledge of your actions, and allow you to escape before the authorities arrive. You'll just be some . . . plausible con man, who fooled me into vouching for you.'

'You know I can't afford to be identified,' I said.

'Then don't get caught.' The Colonel drew himself up to his full height, making it clear the conversation was over. 'I have a limousine standing by to take you to Cardavan House. If you'll just give me your current address . . .'

He stopped, because I was already shaking my head. 'Not going to happen. Just give me directions on how to find the place.'

He nodded stiffly, then handed me an envelope. I thrust it inside my jacket without looking.

'You always have to be your own man, don't you?' said the Colonel.

'Always,' I said. 'It's how I stay alive.'

The Colonel turned on his heel with military precision, and strode off through the Egyptian rooms with his head held high. Very much the man in charge; even though he'd just been forced to beg for a favour from a subordinate. I considered making a rude gesture after him, but it would have felt too much like kicking a man when he was down. And I only do that when there's no other way to win a fight. I waited till I was sure he was gone, and then raised my voice.

'All right, you can come out now.'

The lid on the standing sarcophagus slid jerkily to one side, and Penny Belcourt emerged from it with lissom grace. She smiled dazzlingly.

'He really isn't very observant, is he? And not terribly smart, thinking he could keep me out of this!'

She struck a pose for me: Penny the part-time secret agent. A glamorous presence in her late twenties, she was all dark flashing eyes, trim figure, and enough nervous energy to run the London Underground for a month. She had a pretty face with good bone structure, and a mass of dark hair piled up on top of her head – somewhat flattened at the moment from having to hide inside a coffin too small for her. People were a lot shorter in Ancient Egypt. I blame the diet.

'How long have you been in there?' I said.

'Oh, absolutely ages, darling! I followed your instructions and got here well in advance.'

'How did you avoid being herded away with the others?'

'I just waited till the cameras shut down, then stepped smartly inside the sarcophagus while the guards busied themselves clearing everyone out. They were all in such a hurry that no one noticed a thing.' She beamed around her. 'Why have I never been here before? I love mummies!' Then she stopped and looked at me sharply. 'Why did you agree to take the case? I mean it's not official, you almost certainly won't get paid, and you have no idea how much trouble you'll be getting into.'

'He needs my help,' I said.

'Well, yes,' said Penny. 'That is very sweet and very you, darling, but you must know he hasn't told you everything. His kind never does. I wouldn't be at all surprised if it turned out to be some kind of trap. A chance to watch you in action close up, so he can figure out how you do what you do. And just maybe . . . find out what you really are.'

'The best way to deal with a trap is to know you're walking into one,' I said. 'I have no doubt it'll all turn out to be a lot more complicated than the Colonel said. Families always are. So I shall just have to be even more careful than usual. If I had turned him down, you can be sure he'd be even more impossible to deal with in the future. And besides . . .'

'He needs your help and you couldn't say no.'

'That's right,' I said.

'Every now and again, Ishmael, you remind

18

me of why I love you so much.' She kissed me thoroughly and then beamed around her. 'I had no idea there was so much here. I love mummy films!'

I couldn't help smiling. 'The real thing is very different from what you see in the movies. Ancient Egyptian mummies had all their insides taken out and were basically nothing more than empty shells. Most ended up as little more than glorified body bags with a stylized mask on top. So they couldn't have gone walkabout anyway.'

Penny looked at me. 'I had no idea you were so well informed.'

'I know something about everything,' I said. 'Comes with the job and the territory. I can't take the movies seriously. The mummies always shuffle along so slowly they couldn't catch a snail with a limp and a bad cough. And what makes them so strong, given that they're just old dead things wrapped in bandages? I don't believe in tanna leaves or mystical energies, or ancient sciences long lost to us.'

Penny cut me off with a look. 'You've never encountered a walking mummy?'

'No,' I said.

'You won't even accept the possibility of a reanimated mummy?'

'Not going to happen,' I said. 'Not unless someone unzips one and stuffs it full of clockwork.'

'I believe in some things just because I choose to,' said Penny defiantly. 'Because they make the world so much more interesting! Is there anything more romantic than reincarnated lovers trying to find each other again despite being separated for

19

centuries? Old emotions blossoming in new hearts, souls scattered across time . . . I suppose you don't believe in reincarnation either?'

'I've never come across any evidence to support that theory,' I said carefully. 'And there's nothing romantic about anything in this place. Tomb raiders are really nothing more than grave robbers. Even the ancient dead should have the right to be left to rest in peace, undisturbed.'

'Given the sheer amount of weird shit you've bumped into and occasionally beaten up down the years, I never fail to be amazed by the strange gaps in what you're prepared to accept,' said Penny. 'I still haven't got over finding out you don't believe in ghosts. Everybody believes in ghosts!'

'I'm not everybody. I don't believe in any form of risen dead.'

'But . . . you killed a vampire!'

'Could have been something that just acted like a vampire.'

'Ishmael . . .!'

'There is one thing I am sure of, and one thing only,' I said firmly. 'That dead is dead. In fact, the success of many of my missions has depended on things staying dead after I've killed them.'

'But what if there are levels of death?' Penny said cunningly.

'If it isn't completely dead, it isn't dead.'

Penny folded her arms and glared at me challengingly. 'What is your position on the supernatural?'

'No such thing,' I said immediately. 'There's just the paranormal – extreme forms of science we don't properly understand. Yet.'

Penny shook her head. 'Denial really isn't just a river in Egypt.'

'Sometimes I have no idea what you're talking about.'

'I know!'

I gestured expansively at the exhibits surrounding us. 'There's no denying the old-time Egyptians believed in some pretty weird stuff, but they were capable of surprisingly sophisticated thinking. They believed in a single god, Ra, centuries before Christianity. They also believed in the *ka* – the idea that the conscious mind, or soul, existed as a separate thing from the body. And that this disembodied consciousness could sometimes overwhelm a living mind and drive it out, so the *ka* could live on in a new body.'

'Are we talking about possession?' said Penny.

'It's a very old idea,' I said.

'What about the famous curse?' said Penny, with the air of a card-player slapping down an ace. '*Death shall come on swift wings* . . . and all that?'

'You mean the curse supposedly attached to Howard Carter and his team after they opened Tutankhamun's tomb back in 1922? Complete nonsense. There were any number of investigations into those stories – both at the time and later – and while some people did die, it was always confirmed to be from natural causes. No suspicious circumstances, no signs of supernatural intervention. It was all just stories, Penny. Made up to sell newspapers and please a public fascinated by Egypt's mysterious past.'

21

'How do you know so much about it?' said Penny, suspiciously.

'I read,' I said. 'I have a lot of time to read, in my solitary life.'

Penny stepped in close, and put a gentle hand on my cheek. 'You know I'm with you as much as I can be, Ishmael. As much as you'll let me.'

'I know,' I said.

'You won't let me get too close because you don't want to put me in danger?'

'Yes.'

She stepped back and looked at me sternly. 'You must stop trying to protect me! I am perfectly capable of looking after myself!'

'I know that.'

'You're afraid I might walk away and leave you alone again,' said Penny. 'Don't be. I'm in this for the long haul.'

What I thought but didn't say was that one day I might have to leave her – by living on after she'd died. I have had to do that before, and it never gets any easier.

'Why are you doing this, Ishmael?' asked Penny, deliberately changing the subject. 'I mean, really?'

'It's a chance to put the Colonel in my debt, against future need.'

'Ah! That's more like it!'

'And because he needs my help.'

'You're too good for this world,' said Penny.

Two
In a Dark Place

Cardavan House turned out to be a really long way from anywhere. After hours of hard driving, Penny and I were passing through open countryside so desolate and deserted it felt like another planet. We had the narrow country road all to ourselves as evening fell and the light dropped out of the world. I hadn't seen a tree in ages, and wide empty fields had fallen away behind us, replaced by endless stretches of moorland. Too grim and grey even to make good grazing land, the moors lay flat and sullen under the darkening sky, occasionally interrupted by wet slumps of mire and stunted vegetation. A place where nothing lived because nothing wanted to.

The road punched through bleak and empty land in a perfectly straight line, with no turn-offs for as far as the eye could see. As if our intended destination had decided to make itself inevitable. The street lights had chosen to stay behind when we left the last village, and the car pressed on through the gathering gloom in its own small pool of light. The only sound was the steady roar of the car's engine. The radio had given up the ghost some time back, and I didn't feel like playing any music. If something bad was heading our way, I wanted to be able to hear it coming.

It felt like we'd left civilization behind, to come to a cold and empty place that wanted nothing to do with us.

Penny was driving, because it was her car and she wanted to show off what it could do. She'd developed a taste for vintage cars, and was constantly trading in one model for another as her enthusiasms waxed and waned. Penny inherited a small fortune after both her parents were murdered, and seemed intent on throwing it all away as fast as possible. That was the first case we worked on together. I took down the killer, but not before a lot of people died. Penny never held that against me. But I did.

Her latest pride and joy was a powder-blue Hillman Super Minx convertible. The engine roared like a caged beast every time she put her foot down, but after being stuck behind the wheel for so long Penny had run out of enthusiasm and now she just concentrated fiercely on the road ahead. I'd been glad to leave the city behind. Penny was an aggressive driver in traffic, disputing the right of way with taxis and buses – which was not something they were used to – and given to shouting 'Get out of the bloody way!' at anyone with the temerity to drive where she wanted to be. While I sank right down in my seat and pretended I wasn't there.

'Are you sure we're following the Colonel's directions properly?' Penny said abruptly. 'I mean, I haven't seen you look at them once.'

'That's because I memorized them before we left,' I said patiently. 'And I haven't given you any directions in ages because this is the only

24

road there is. No turnings, no surprises, not even a pothole to break the monotony. We should be seeing a sign up ahead sometime soon, pointing down a private road that will take us straight to Cardavan House.'

'I don't see a sign anywhere in this bloody wilderness,' said Penny, glaring ahead into the failing light. 'Why can't we just enter our destination into the satnav? It's got a lovely posh voice that I paid extra for.'

'Only because you fancied the actor who provided it.' I stretched slowly in my seat, though there wasn't enough legroom for that to help much. 'We can't use the satnav, because Cardavan House isn't on any map. The family takes its security very seriously.'

Penny's scowl deepened dangerously. 'We're going to be spending another weekend in another dreary old country house, aren't we? I'm getting really fed up with that. And I'm telling you right now, if people start dying on us again we're leaving!'

'I thought you liked playing ace girl detective,' I said mildly.

'I do! It's just . . . Why can't murders and mysteries ever take place somewhere nice? I mean, really nice.'

'Cardavan House might be nice . . .'

'Look around us!' Penny said savagely. 'This whole area would need decades of economic investment just to qualify as a disaster zone. It's been ages since we left that little village behind, and I can't remember the last time I passed any other traffic on this road.'

'Keep going,' I said. 'Cardavan House can't be far now. If only because if we keep going, we'll run out of world.'

'Why would anyone want to live all the way out here?' said Penny. 'I mean, look at it! There's nothing to look at.'

'People have all kinds of reasons to want to get away from everything,' I said wisely. 'And the Cardavans have more grounds than most. If you owned the world's biggest private collection of valuable Ancient Egyptian artefacts, you'd probably want to put as much distance as possible between you and the authorities. And any of your fellow collectors who might be overcome by jealousy or itchy fingers.'

'Couldn't you at least look at the directions?' Penny pleaded. 'Just for my peace of mind?'

'I can't,' I said. 'I burned them before we left.'

'*You did what?*' The car lurched worryingly for a moment, before Penny got herself under control again. 'Why would you do that?'

'The Colonel's instructions. Burn after reading. Very security conscious, our Colonel. As, presumably, are the Cardavans.'

'They'd better have a mummy,' Penny said darkly. 'Only a proper mummy with a mysterious background and a really nasty death curse attached could make this journey worthwhile. I mean, I love mummies but . . .'

'You mean you love the movies,' I said. 'Watching Hollywood movies to learn about mummies is like watching James Bond films to get an idea of what it would be like working for MI6.'

'You like mummy movies too!'

'Sometimes,' I said. 'I liked the opening sequence in the Boris Karloff film. Very atmospheric. And I did like the one with Christopher Lee and Peter Cushing. Classic Hammer horror.'

'I prefer the ones with Brendan Fraser,' said Penny. 'They're more like . . . romantic adventures.'

I had to smile. 'When it comes to historical accuracy, I think the producers of those films decided very early on that wasn't something they wanted anything to do with . . . *There's the sign!*'

The simple wooden sign jumped into the car's headlights so suddenly we almost missed the turning. Penny stamped on the brake and swung the wheel hard round, the gear box making horrid noises as she crashed through the gears. I clung on grimly as we took the sharp curve on what felt like two wheels, and then we were roaring down another perfectly straight road.

Two large gates of heavy black iron stood open before us, and Penny blasted between them without even slowing. I was actually a little relieved at this indication that we were on the right road at last. And then felt a little less relieved, as it occurred to me no one should have known we were there. I couldn't believe the security-conscious Cardavans would leave their front gates standing open until we just happened to turn up. Even as I thought this, the gates smoothly swung shut behind us. Either to keep the world out or keep us in. Someone was watching us. And I am never comfortable with that.

'OK,' said Penny, glancing in the rear-view mirror. 'That was just a little bit creepy.'

'It's all about security,' I said. 'I feel very secure now, don't you?'

'I lost all feeling in my bottom ages ago,' Penny said grimly. 'The sooner we can get out of this car and collapse into something comfortable, preferably with a large drink in both hands, the better.'

The road became a gravel path, plunging through what seemed like acres of open grounds. No trees or hedges, no flower displays or lawn ornaments, nothing to show anybody lived here or gave a damn about their surroundings. The steady roar of the car was the only disturbance on the hushed evening air, as though the very landscape resented us being there.

We drove for some time before Cardavan House finally loomed up ahead of us, standing tall and solid in its own massive pool of dazzling security lights. The Cardavans really didn't want anyone sneaking up on them. Penny actually let out a brief cry of relief; but I wasn't so sure. The house had a cold and forbidding aspect, more like a fortress than a home. It was square and blocky, almost brutal in its aesthetics. Three stories high, it looked like it had been built to keep people out, rather than nourish those within. Only a few lights showed at the many windows, all of them on the ground floor.

There was nothing welcoming about the house. It looked like it had been dropped here in the middle of nowhere because nowhere else would have it. Just looking at the building made my skin crawl. It felt . . . spiritually unhealthy, as though the life within it had soured and gone off.

'You're frowning,' said Penny. 'Which is rarely a good sign. Should I be thinking seriously about turning the car round and making a run for it?'

'No,' I said. 'I promised the Colonel I'd help. But I have to say I'm worried about this family he's married into. How could anything good thrive in a place like this?'

'It does have a certain oppressive, even soul-destroying quality,' said Penny. 'Could it be Sick Building Syndrome?'

'More like Put this Unnatural Thing out of its Misery Syndrome,' I said.

'Last chance to get the hell out of Dodge, sweetie.'

'No. We go on.'

Penny started singing the theme from the old Addams Family TV show, taking both hands off the steering wheel to do the finger snaps.

When we finally reached the end of the long gravel road, the Colonel was there waiting for us. Standing stiffly in front of the main entrance, as though silently reprimanding us for being late. Penny brought the car to a sweeping halt right in front of him, shooting loose gravel in all directions. The Colonel didn't even flinch. Penny shut down the engine with a flourish, and then leant over the steering wheel with an exaggerated groan of relief. I got out of the car, looked quickly around to assure myself the area was as empty as I thought it was, and then nodded to the

Colonel. Penny half fell out of the driving seat, swore loudly, and slammed the door shut. She stretched her back, and vigorously massaged her backside with both hands.

'If I'd known it was going to take this long, I'd have hired a chauffeur!'

'Next time, I'll drive,' I said.

'Not one of my cars, you won't. I've seen you drive.'

'I'm an excellent driver.'

'It's sweet that you think that.'

We stood together before the Colonel, presenting a unified front in the face of an authority figure. He nodded briefly to both of us, entirely unmoved by anything he'd seen or heard. He looked positively imperious in his formal tuxedo, while still maintaining the casual style necessary to carry off such a look. He sniffed disparagingly at my casual black leather jacket and battered jeans, but managed a small smile for Penny's powder-blue trouser suit. Chosen to match her car. She gave the Colonel a challenging look.

'Didn't expect to see me here, did you?'

'I had hoped Mister Jones would take the hint and come alone,' the Colonel said calmly, 'But I gave up expecting him to do the reasonable thing long ago. I told the Cardavans to expect both of you. Try not to embarrass me in front of the family.'

'How did you know to be out here to meet us?' I said. 'I didn't see any security guards in the grounds.'

'There aren't any guards,' said the Colonel. 'The current head of the family doesn't believe in them. He prefers extensive electronic surveillance; in the grounds, the perimeter, and most of the surrounding roads. We knew you were coming before you even approached the gates. How else do you think we knew to open them for you?'

'Do the Cardavans really have that many enemies?' said Penny.

'There's nothing like owning a major private collection to make you very concerned about all the people who might want to take it away from you,' said the Colonel.

'I didn't see any cameras,' I said. 'And you know I have more experience than most when it comes to spotting such things.'

'They're very well hidden. Don't worry, after you've left there won't be any record of your being here. Because officially you never were.'

'Story of my life,' I said.

Penny bestowed her most dazzling smile on the Colonel. 'You're looking very splendid in your tux, Colonel. If I'd known we were dressing formally for dinner, I'd have packed a more extensive wardrobe.'

I gave her a hard look. 'You already packed everything short of the wardrobe. I strained my back trying to force all your cases into the boot and the back seat. We're only here for the weekend!'

'A girl likes to have choices when it comes to looking her best,' Penny said airily. She smiled at the Colonel again. 'Ignore Ishmael. He's just being Mister Grumpy.'

'You can leave your cases in the entrance hall,' said the Colonel. 'I want you to meet the family before you go up to your room. It's important you make a good first impression, Mister Jones.'

'Sorry,' I said. 'I don't do that.'

'It's true,' said Penny. 'He really doesn't.'

'Try,' said the Colonel.

I looked at him thoughtfully. 'Anything I should know about before we go in? Any surprises, or changes in the situation?'

'Nothing you can't cope with,' said the Colonel. 'Just try to remember why you're here.'

'Show me the mummy,' I said.

The Colonel escorted Penny through the main door and into the entrance hall, while I struggled with the suitcases. One for me, and three for Penny. Fortunately, I'm a lot stronger than most people. I dropped the cases in the hall and kicked the door shut behind me. It produced a satisfyingly loud crash but the Colonel didn't flinch, even as the echoes rumbled on. He was too busy showing off some of the house's more interesting features to Penny.

The entrance hall was long, high-ceilinged and disturbingly gloomy. Electric bulbs blazed in widely spaced chandeliers, but the light didn't spread far enough to make much of an impression. Shadows lurked everywhere, as though waiting for a chance to sneak up on us. There was nothing in the least welcoming about the entrance hall; but that was hardly a surprise after seeing the exterior. Cardavan House was there for the family, no one else.

Penny interrupted the Colonel's lecture to gesture at the shadows and smile sweetly.

'Are you having trouble with the electricity, Colonel?'

'No,' he said. 'The current head of the family likes it this way. George believes in maintaining a suitable atmosphere. It's all about what's best for the collection.'

I didn't need to be told that. The Cardavan collection was already making its presence felt. Glass display cases with polished wood trimmings lined the whole length of the hall, packed with pottery, small statues, scarabs and reliquaries, and all the usual Ancient Egyptian bits and pieces. The leftovers and cultural debris of a vanished civilization. Once again, cat heads were everywhere, smiling their inscrutable smiles and regarding me suspiciously with unblinking eyes. Various papyrus scrolls covered in row upon row of hieroglyphics had been carefully unrolled and stretched out, under heavy glass of course, across the walls. I'd taught myself to read some of it before I left, enough to fake it in company. Typical of the Cardavans to have the world's most expensive wallpaper.

I moved slowly forward, peering into one display case after another. Dozens of clay stelae had been set out on plump purple velvet, in no particular order. I recognized some of the symbols etched or stamped on them. Nothing important or surprising; business records, mostly. But just seeing so many in one place was enough to convince me there was no way they could have got here legally.

I ended up standing before a sarcophagus that had been leant nonchalantly against the wall, beside a battered grandfather clock. An ancient relic, set next to a more modern one. Penny and the Colonel came to stand on either side of me as I leaned in for a closer look at the coffin lid. The golden overlay was covered with the most exquisite artwork, the vivid colours barely faded. A full-length portrait of the personage within had been topped with a bas-relief face so stylized as to seem almost inhuman. I glanced at the Colonel.

'Anyone I should have heard of?'

'The occupant of this particular sarcophagus was called Nesmin,' said the Colonel. 'He's not in there now, the coffin is empty. Down the years, mummy and case passed through many hands, bringing bad luck and disaster to one and all. Until the previous owner decided enough was enough and had the mummy burned. Reduced to ashes . . . which were then dumped in a fast-running river, just in case.'

'Did people have any reason to believe these stories?' I asked.

The Colonel shrugged. 'The Cardavans acquired the empty sarcophagus some time back. It makes for a great conversation piece.'

'And the bad luck?' said Penny.

'Died with the mummy, Miss Belcourt,' said the Colonel. 'Or so they say.'

'Please, call me Penny.' She smiled at him winningly. 'We're all friends here.'

The Colonel didn't appear too convinced, but he inclined his head politely.

'Penny has a point,' I said. 'I can't call you Colonel in front of the Cardavans. So Penny is Penny, I am Ishmael . . . and you are?'

34

'Stuart March,' said the Colonel, staring determinedly at the sarcophagus.

'Stuart . . . Yes, that works,' said Penny.

'It's very you, Stuart,' I said solemnly.

'It's going to be a long weekend,' said the Colonel.

He led us further into Cardavan House, down one gloomy corridor after another. I had to fight to keep from pulling a face. The air was increasingly saturated with rich, heavy scents, powerful enough to swamp my sense of smell. Spices, preservatives and chemicals hit me from every direction at once, until I had no choice but to dial down my sense of smell to the point where it was all but useless. Being able to detect scents other people couldn't had saved my life on more than one occasion and I had to wonder . . . had this been specially arranged, just for me? But who in this place would know enough about me to do that? Even the Colonel didn't know; or at least, he shouldn't. Penny picked up on my discomfort, and put a questioning hand on my arm. I gave her a quick shake of the head behind the Colonel's back, indicating that we'd talk about it later.

'Why isn't there a butler, Stuart?' Penny said quickly. 'With a house this size, I would have expected a full uniformed staff, all of them fighting each other to minister to our every need.'

'Normally, there would be,' said the Colonel. Or Stuart, as I had to think of him now. 'But they've all been given the weekend off, since this is to be a private gathering to celebrate George's

35

new acquisition. So we'll just have to rough it and look after ourselves.'

'How will we ever survive?' I murmured.

'How did you come to be part of this family, Stuart?' said Penny, glaring at me. 'I mean, we need to know the background if we're to make sense of the case.'

Stuart slowed his pace, falling back so he could walk beside Penny and me. He stared straight ahead, his gaze giving nothing away, and when he spoke he seemed to be addressing some unseen audience rather than me or Penny. His tone was calm and casual. He could have been talking about anyone.

'I was orphaned at an early age, and passed from one distant relative to another like an unwanted obligation. The moment I was old enough, I was sent to public school. Holidays were a nightmare. Just one place after another. I never felt like I belonged anywhere, because I was never made to feel like I belonged. I joined the Army the moment I left school, just to annoy my family. The one place I could be sure they couldn't touch me.'

'That's so sad,' said Penny.

'Not a bit of it,' Stuart said briskly. 'The Army was the making of me. The regimental history gave me my first sense of being part of something greater than myself, and the Army became the first real family I'd ever known. And you get to take out your frustrations on people who you are firmly assured fit all the necessary criteria for "bad guys". I liked having orders to follow, and people to give orders to.'

'Imagine my surprise,' I murmured.

36

'I was happy in the Army,' said Stuart. 'I never wanted to leave . . . but I was wounded in action. In a country we weren't officially supposed to be in. Rather than be stuck behind a desk, pushing papers around, I chose to resign my commission. I'd barely swapped my uniform for an ill-fitting suit when I was approached by Black Heir. I'd been through some unusual experiences during that last military action, and someone had been impressed by how I'd dealt with things.'

'How did you deal with them?' I said.

'Firmly,' said Stuart. Still not looking at me. 'Someone in the Army put in a word on my behalf and I was invited to join Black Heir. Which turned out to be very like the Army, if you stretch the definition of "bad guys" to its limits.'

'They have a way of doing that,' I said.

'I met Chloe when we both worked for Black Heir. The Cardavans took me in once they realized I had no one else and made me part of the family. I've always been very grateful to them for that. Let me make myself clear to both of you. Whatever happens this weekend, whatever we discover . . . I want Chloe and her family protected.'

'In that order?' I said.

He looked at me for the first time. 'Yes.'

'How did you end up in the Organization?' said Penny.

'The same way everyone does,' said Stuart. 'They decided they wanted me.'

He increased his pace and left us behind. Penny and I looked at each other.

'A lot about that man makes more sense now,' said Penny.

'I don't know,' I said. 'He didn't tell us anything I hadn't already worked out for myself. Chloe is the only new thing.'

'He opened up to us,' said Penny. 'Showed us his vulnerable side.'

'Did he?' I said. 'To me, he seems more dangerous than ever. Because we now know he's got someone he'll fight for.'

Stuart stopped before a closed door at the end of a particularly long corridor, and waited till we caught up with him.

'Wait here,' he said. 'I need to have a few words with the family before I introduce you.'

'Why?' I said. 'We're not that scary.'

'They are,' said Stuart.

He opened the door and went in, closing the door firmly in our faces. And I had to wonder whether he was preparing the family to meet us or warning them about me.

'If he's so happy to be part of this family,' said Penny, 'why does he think they're scary?'

'Have you seen the house they live in?' I said. 'It's enough to give the Addams family panic attacks and chronic bed wetting. And anyway, all families can be scary, depending on the secrets they keep from each other.'

'You've never had a family,' said Penny. 'You're an orphan, just like him.'

'No,' I said. 'I'm nothing like him.'

'Oh, come on, Ishmael. He's not the enemy. He opened up to us! He didn't have to do that.'

'No, he didn't,' I said. 'Which makes me wonder why he did.'

'Maybe being here relaxes him.'

'Among his scary family? Besides, I don't think that man knows how to relax. Probably sleeps at attention. He brought us here to do something for him; something that needs doing, that he can't do himself. And, possibly, something he can blame on me. Everything he just told us could be nothing more than part of the softening up process. Make us think we know him, so he can catch us off guard.'

'You are undoubtedly the most cynical person I have ever known,' said Penny. 'And I've worked in publishing.'

'Don't blame me,' I said. 'Blame life.'

'Your life, possibly.'

The door swung open suddenly, and there was Stuart beckoning for us to enter. I strode past him as though he was just the butler, and nodded easily to one and all. Penny strode along with me, one arm firmly linked through mine, favouring everyone with her most dazzling smile. The room before us was laid out and decorated on the grand scale. It could have been a living room, a drawing room or even a small ballroom. It was big enough to host a major Olympic event and still have enough room left over for a dwarf-throwing contest. Bright lights from yet more chandeliers forced the shadows back into the corners, but couldn't eliminate them completely.

All four walls were lined with shelves, weighed down with even more Ancient Egyptian treasure trove. At least the room's furniture was reassuringly modern. The Cardavans stood together, studying Penny and me thoughtfully. It only took me a moment to realize they were arranged in

39

four separate couples, rather than one gathering. The gaps between the couples were small but significant, suggesting a family with deep emotional divisions. For me, body language is always an open book. Stuart closed the door and came forward to make the introductions.

'Ishmael Jones, Penny Belcourt. May I present to you George Cardavan and his wife Marjorie?'

George was clearly the alpha male of the family. I could tell from the way he held himself – ready and eager to fight off any threat or competition. A large, blocky middle-aged man, he dominated the room through practised belligerence and wore his expensive tweed suit as though he felt it was expected of him. He had one of those square bullish faces, that I just knew would flush angrily if anyone dared contradict him. His handshake was brief, but crushing. When I didn't wince he nodded approvingly, as though I'd passed some kind of test. He smiled briefly at Penny, but didn't offer her his hand.

Alpha male. Go-getter. Probably a bit of a bully, too. I gave him my best meaningless smile.

The young woman at his side had all the trappings of a second wife. Barely half her husband's age, Marjorie had a frankly magnificent body, lots of blonde hair, and clothes that shrieked of money if not style. She was pretty in a characterless way, as though it was something she'd copied from a magazine, and wore the kind of make-up designed to be seen clearly across a crowded room. She dripped jewellery at every conceivable point, as if to say 'Look how much my man loves me! He gave me all this!' Her wide smile didn't even come close to reaching her eyes, and she didn't offer to shake hands. She clung possessively to George's arm, as if to say 'Look what I caught!' and 'He belongs to me now'.

Trophy wife. All the determination of a bulldog, and almost as much charm.

'Welcome to my home, Ishmael,' said George. 'So, you're Stuart's pet expert. He speaks very highly of you. Can't wait to hear what you have to say about my mummy.' He let out a brief bark of laughter. 'My mummy, my show, my way. Remember that and we'll get along fine.'

'You and your silly collection,' Marjorie said artlessly. 'At least offer the man a drink before you start to pressure him.'

'I'd like one too,' said Penny.

'What will you have?' said George, rubbing his hands together in that way people do when they like to think they know how to make cocktails. 'If you can pour it and mix it, I've got it here somewhere.'

I asked for a brandy, Penny for a gin and tonic. George bustled over to the old-fashioned bar to do manly things with bottles and glasses. Booze doesn't actually do anything for me, but I find people relax around me more if they see me drinking. Marjorie went with her husband, rather than be left alone with Penny and me.

Stuart presented us to his wife, Chloe. His usual clipped tones softened perceptibly as he introduced her, and she smiled fondly at him before turning her smile on me. Her handshake was brief but firm, and felt a lot more like the real thing. A tall striking brunette in her thirties, she wore

41

a silk cocktail dress. And very high heels, to make her the same height as her husband. She accentuated her thin lips with scarlet lipstick, but otherwise didn't bother with make-up. Her eyes were dark and sparkling, and she stood very close to Stuart.

'You probably need a good rest after such a long drive,' Chloe said pleasantly. 'But you can bet Daddy will make you look at his precious mummy first. It's all he thinks about these days. Just smile and nod and get it over with, and then you can go up to your room for a nice lie down before dinner.'

'Ishmael knows his business,' said Stuart. 'I'm sure he's just dying to see the mummy.'

'Can't wait,' I said. 'I've brought a special stick to poke it with.'

Chloe gave me an uncertain look, and then she and Stuart stepped back so we could meet George's son, Nicholas. He didn't seem too inter-ested in meeting us, but his wife urged him forward. Broad and stocky like his father, Nicholas was in his late twenties, but a certain childish sulkiness undermined any impression he might have made. He slumped inside his expensive suit, as though he couldn't be bothered to live up to it. A weak chin, a petulant mouth, and a constant scowl seemed to make up his entire character. He couldn't be bothered to shake hands, just growled in my general direction and brooded over the large drink in his hand.

Youngest child. No longer indulged. Only here under protest.

Nicholas's wife, Caroline, had enough character

for both of them. A hard-faced blonde with a direct gaze and an overbearing voice, she was almost aggressively cheerful. She'd dressed to impress, and taste be damned. She insisted on shaking my hand, with a lingering touch, and then kissed the air somewhere near Penny's cheeks before quickly turning back to give me her full attention.

'Welcome to Cardavan House! Dreadful old dump, isn't it? Ugly as sin, but not nearly as much fun. Nicholas can't stand the place. But here we are again, to spend a long weekend in a draughty room with a toilet at the far end of the corridor. Still, needs must when the master calls. Especially when he's got a new wife.' She leaned in close. 'Nicholas's mother died very suddenly. It was a blow to all of us. Only one in the family I had any time for. George was so upset he got married again just a few months later. We were all shocked, if not particularly surprised. Are you really an expert on this Egyptian nonsense? You don't look old enough to be an expert. But then it all looks like junk to me. Still, as long as it's worth serious money, I am prepared to appear suitably interested. Have to keep an eye on Nicky's inheritance! That's what I always say. Don't I, Nicky?'

She stopped talking just long enough to give him a sharp look, perhaps to make sure he was paying attention. He just grunted. Caroline turned back to resume her charm offensive, but I had already steered Penny away. It's not running away if it's self-defence. I got the feeling Caroline was best appreciated in small doses.

The final couple consisted of George's father, Bernard, and his wife, Susan. Bernard had to be in his late seventies, and looked older. His face was heavily lined, his hair had disappeared, he stooped, and his hands trembled. There was an odd vagueness to his gaze and his attention seemed to drift even as I introduced myself, before snapping suddenly back again. He was still a large and blocky man, like his son, but his clothes hung loosely about him, as though made for a somewhat larger man. He nodded brusquely, and made no attempt to shake hands.

It's always sad when the leader of the pack is replaced by a younger alpha male.

Bernard's wife, Susan, clung to his arm at all times, partly in support and partly to make sure he stayed where he was supposed to be. A pleasant enough sort, with a kind if worn face and tightly permed grey hair. She tried to look cheerful, but was too tired to be convincing. She rarely took her eyes off Bernard, as though she felt the need to constantly reassure herself that everything was all right with him.

I know a carer when I see one.

George came back with our drinks, and thrust them into my hand and Penny's. Big glasses, big drinks. Not because he was generous, but because he always needed to impress. He talked straight at me, because anything he had to say was always going to be more important than anything I might come up with.

'Cardavan House used to belong to my father,' he said bluntly. 'Now it's mine. I took control, for the good of the family. Bit of a shame, but it had to be done. Father let the family fortune go to pot. I took care of that. And now I run the house, the family, and the family collection.' He paused, to fix me with a steely gaze. 'Stuart tells me you used to work for Black Heir. Chloe did too. She told me all about it. That's how I came up with the idea for my business.'

'Even though she wasn't supposed to,' murmured Stuart. He'd drifted casually back to join us, with Chloe still sticking close. George just talked right over his son-in-law.

'I spotted a gap in the market, saw where I could make myself useful, and Black Heir was happy to have me do it. For the right price, of course. I put this family back on its feet in under three years.'

I glanced across at Bernard. He didn't look particularly impressed, or grateful.

'So,' I said to George, 'the collection is yours now?'

'Someone has to look after it,' said George.

'How did you and Marjorie meet?' said Penny.

'I was George's secretary,' said Marjorie, moving in beside her husband. Determined not to be left out of anything.

I spotted some significant glances between various members of the family, but no one said anything.

'I moved back into the house when I took control of the family,' said George, not even glancing at Bernard. 'Mother and father still live here, of course.'

Bernard didn't look too happy about that, either. His hands were shaking more now, possibly with suppressed rage. Susan made him sit down in a comfortable chair, and put a fresh drink in his hand. He held it loosely, as though he wasn't sure what it was for. Susan came forward to join us, lowering her voice confidentially.

'He isn't supposed to drink, not with all the medication he takes, but it helps calm him down.'

'He's not well, is he?' I said.

'Not really, no,' said Susan. 'I do my best to keep the peace between him and George because, well . . .'

'Because it's either that or a nursing home,' said George, not bothering to lower his voice. 'He's got Alzheimer's. Don't look at me like that, mother, it's hardly a secret. He had it for some time, but wouldn't admit it. Which is why I had to come in and restore the family fortunes, after he pissed them away.'

'George!' said Susan. She didn't get an apology, and didn't look like she expected one. She smiled wearily at me. 'Bernard is more himself in familiar surroundings.'

She excused herself and went back to her husband to murmur soothing words he didn't seem to hear.

'She's devoted to him,' said Chloe. 'Though I sometimes wonder why. He can be . . . a bit much.'

'Because that's how wives are supposed to be!' said George. He looked to Marjorie to agree with him, and scowled when he found she'd wandered away to freshen her drink. He went after her, to make sure she didn't do anything he wouldn't approve of. I looked at Stuart, but he didn't say anything. Penny smiled brightly at Chloe.

'Stuart hasn't told us much about you. Even though we've been working together for some time. What's he really like, when he isn't working?'

'Oh, Stuart's a sweetie,' said Chloe, taking her husband's hand in hers as though it belonged there. 'Can't do enough for me.'

'And vice versa, of course,' said Stuart.

I barely recognized the look on his face. I wasn't used to seeing the Colonel appear so . . . at ease.

Chloe smiled at me. An oddly challenging smile. 'Stuart hasn't told me much about your background, Ishmael. You were with Black Heir?'

'For a time,' I said. 'These days, my expertise is called upon by many groups of a confidential nature.'

'Oh, one of those,' said Chloe. 'Hush-hush. Don't ask, don't tell. And don't even bother to remember your name because officially you were never here.'

'Exactly,' I said.

'Maybe you can answer a question for me,' Penny said to Chloe. 'Since neither Ishmael nor Stuart seem able to. Black Heir exists to clean up after starship crashes, of which there never seems to be any shortage. Now these ships must be marvels of advanced technology to be able to cross untold light years of space to get here, but the moment they enter our atmosphere everything goes to pot and they end up falling out of the sky like Autumn leaves. Why?'

'People have been asking that question for a long time,' said Chloe. 'Our best guess is there's a war going on out there.'

'You mean they came all this way just to shoot at each other?'

'Presumably they have their reasons,' said Chloe. 'We're learning more and more about their tech, but we still don't know much about them.'

'Which them?' said Penny.

'Any of them,' said Stuart.

The door behind us opened suddenly, and everyone turned to stare at the new arrival. A quiet, scholarly gentleman in his forties, he had a great shock of prematurely grey hair, a thin face and a beaked nose. The suit he was wearing didn't even try to be the equal of everyone else's. The jacket had leather patches on the elbows. The newcomer smiled diffidently about him.

'I heard voices, so I assumed the new expert had arrived. Mister Jones? How nice to meet you.' He inclined his head slightly, but that was all. 'Ishmael Jones . . . What an interesting name. Not one I know, and I thought I had heard of everyone in my field. Everyone of note, at least.'

No one butts heads like scholars defending their territory.

'My work is nearly always confidential,' I said. 'People only know about me if they need to.'

'Professor Samuel Rose,' George said loudly, 'is my very own personal expert. More qualifications than you can shake a mortar board at, and more experience with Ancient Egyptian relics than anyone else. I know. I checked. If there had been anyone better, I'd have hired them. The

48

professor is here to catalogue my collection. Because it hasn't been properly looked at and assessed in far too long. I want to know everything there is to know about everything I've got. And its worth, down to the very last penny.'

'For the insurance?' Penny said sweetly.

'Hardly,' said George. 'Can't have outsiders in here, asking officious questions about what I've got and where it came from. No, I don't ever intend to sell any of it. I just want to know.'

'Your father was in charge of the collection before you,' I said carefully. 'Didn't he keep a record?'

'Father hasn't been on top of things for some time,' said George.

'Aren't you concerned the professor will tell the world what you've got here?' said Penny.

'We have a deal,' said George. 'The professor gets to examine a collection no one else has ever seen and write a book about it, but he doesn't get to say who owns it or where it is. Our contract has more confidentiality and penalty clauses than a Hollywood pre-nup.'

'It's worth it,' Rose said calmly. 'For the chance to examine a collection of this magnitude.'

No one apart from George seemed at all interested in the professor. He clearly hadn't been invited to this little get-together. He was just here to do a job, like one of the servants. It didn't seem to bother the professor. He just smiled easily at everyone . . . and showed no intention of leaving.

'What do you think of the collection, Professor?' said Penny.

49

He smiled warmly, and his voice took on a quiet enthusiasm. 'The Cardavan collection contains little that is particularly rare or truly significant . . . but the sheer size helps to make clear trends and practices that could shed a whole new light on entire periods of Egyptian history.'

'Like this new Cleopatra?' said Penny.

'Exactly,' said Rose.

'But if no one apart from you gets to see it . . .' I said.

'It all adds to the sum of historical knowledge,' Rose said firmly. 'My book will be the definitive work.'

'To what end?' I said.

He looked down his prominent nose at me. 'Knowledge is its own end, Mister Jones. I would have expected an expert of your magnitude to know that.'

'Mister Jones is here at my invitation,' said Stuart. 'Specifically, he is here to authenticate the mummy to my satisfaction.'

Rose bridled for the first time, drawing himself up to his full height. Though he didn't have far to go. 'I have already done so, and I would have thought my background and expertise would be more than sufficient to satisfy anyone.' He glared at me coldly. 'What exactly is your background, Mister Jones? What are your qualifications, your published works?'

Everyone looked at me. I smiled easily back at the professor. 'A condition of my coming here was anonymity. Given some of the organizations I work for, no one gets to know anything about me beyond what's necessary. You don't think

Ishmael Jones is my real name, do you? I don't need to convince you of my bona fides, Professor Rose, nor anyone else here. Stuart knows. George can accept my opinion on his mummy or not, as he pleases. I don't see why it should matter to you, Professor. After all, you'll still be here studying the collection and writing your book long after I'm gone.'

Rose nodded stiffly, accepting the point. For now. I looked around at the family. They didn't seem as sure of me as they had before. Stuart cleared his throat, and everyone turned to look at him.

'Mister Jones is my expert,' he said loudly. 'I vouch for him. That should be enough.'

'Well of course it is, dear,' Chloe said quickly. And then she glared round at everyone else.

'Of course, of course,' said George, perhaps just a little too quickly to be entirely convincing.

But there was something in the way he looked at Professor Rose that made me think George liked seeing the professor put in his place. Perhaps because the academic was the only one who knew more about the collection than George did. Rose was just there to do a job, not to get above himself.

'Can I just say I was surprised to find out there are no security guards,' I said to George. 'A bit risky, I would have thought, given the obvious value of your collection.'

Everyone pulled a variety of faces, none of them happy. George's face set into stubborn lines.

'I won't have strangers stomping about the place, getting underfoot. This is still a family home.'

'Is it?' said Bernard. 'I remember when it was my home.'

'Hush, dear,' said Susan.

'Why?' Bernard said loudly. 'Aren't I allowed to speak my own mind any longer?'

'I put my faith in electronic surveillance,' George said firmly. 'Security cameras never get bored or tired, or take breaks. I trust them to watch over what's mine day and night.'

I didn't. Security cameras are only ever as dependable as the people you set to watch them.

'What about burglars?' said Penny.

This time there were pitying looks from pretty much everyone.

'We're miles from everywhere,' said Chloe. 'Surrounded by acres of open land. No one can get anywhere near us without being noticed. We have unbreakable glass in all the windows, and reinforced doors. Though God help us if there's ever a fire . . .'

'We are not installing sprinklers,' George said firmly. 'One false alarm is all it would take to cause untold damage to the collection. There's a smoke alarm and a fire extinguisher in every room. Settle for that.'

'Security here is exceptional,' said Stuart.

I met his eyes for a moment, just to remind him that I would take it very badly if I should turn up on any recordings. He inclined his head, just a little, to show he hadn't forgotten.

'But if there was a problem,' said Penny, still worrying doggedly at the point, 'How long would it take for help to arrive? Given that we are miles from anywhere.'

'Armed security men could be here in under an hour,' said George.

'A lot can happen in an hour,' I said.

'There's no real danger,' said Stuart. 'Most of the items in this collection are so rare they couldn't easily be sold on.'

'What about other private collectors?' I said. 'What are the chances some of them might be jealous enough to want some of these things for themselves? Just so they could have them, and not you?'

There was an awkward pause. Clearly, certain names were suggesting themselves. Even if no one wanted to say them out loud.

'None of them would dare,' George said finally. 'I'd know. I would make it my business to find out. And they all know that. I have the best defence against being robbed – no one dares steal from me for fear of what I'd do to them.'

'Are we the only ones in the house?' I said.

'It's just us, for the weekend,' said Stuart.

George sniffed loudly. 'Damn staff all insisted on having the weekend off. It's the only way you can keep servants these days.'

'Must be a lot of dusting to do around here,' Penny said innocently.

'The collection does take a lot of looking after,' said Chloe. 'We can't allow it to deteriorate.'

'Or depreciate,' said Nicholas, smirking to himself.

'We hold these things in trust,' Chloe said firmly. 'For future generations.'

'Then you'd better get on with producing the next generation, girl,' said George. 'You're not getting any younger, you know.'

'Daddy!' said Chloe.

She didn't blush, just glared at her father, while he smiled at her indulgently. I noticed he didn't say anything to his son, who'd gone back to sulking in the background. Nicholas's wife, Caroline, studied everyone with sharp, calculating eyes.

'What,' I asked, 'would happen to the collection in the event there was no one left in the family who cared about it?'

I didn't look at Nicholas when I said that, but certain other eyes glanced in his direction. He scowled back defiantly, but didn't say anything.

'There are arrangements in place,' said Chloe, 'for all eventualities.'

'Can you trust your security people to keep quiet about the mummy,' I said, 'given how special and newsworthy it is?'

'For what I'm paying them, they'll keep their mouths shut,' George said sharply. 'They know what will happen to anyone who crosses me. And the servants are just here to work. They haven't a clue what anything is.'

We all broke off as Bernard surged up out of his chair. He was scowling in my direction and shook off Susan as she tried to hold him back.

'What's going on here?' he said loudly. 'Who are these people? What are they doing in my home?'

'They're Stuart's guests, grandfather,' Chloe said quickly. 'Ishmael Jones and Penny Belcourt. You met them earlier, remember?'

'Yes, yes,' Bernard said testily. 'I remember them, of course I do. But what are they doing here?'

'They're here to look at my mummy, father,' said George. 'Now sit down and have another drink. Mother, can't you keep him under control?'

Susan ignored him, intent on persuading Bernard to sit down again. He reluctantly did so.

'He's getting worse,' said George.

'He's fine most of the time,' said Chloe. 'And you know it would be cruel to send him away.'

'You're not here all the time, dear,' said Marjorie, just a bit pointedly. 'You don't have to cope with him when he's having one of his turns.'

'Hush, Marjorie,' said George.

'Yes, dear.'

They were all talking as though Bernard couldn't hear them, but of course he could. His large hands had closed into fists. He might understand the necessity of his living conditions, but he didn't have to like it.

'He almost destroyed the family fortunes,' said George. 'I had to take them away from him.'

'It was necessary,' said Chloe. 'We all talked about it for ages.'

'Behind my back!' Bernard said loudly.

'It was for your own good, grandfather,' Chloe said firmly. 'You still have a home here . . .'

Bernard laughed briefly. It was a harsh, bitter sound. He glowered at his son from under heavy brows. 'You couldn't wait to inherit, could you, George? You had to have it all, had to be master of Cardavan House. Couldn't wait till I was decently dead! And you couldn't wait to start cutting back on the business, laying off people who'd worked for this family all their lives. And now I'm just a boarder in my own home . . .'

'You put two mortgages on Cardavan House and then couldn't keep up the payments,' said George, entirely unmoved. 'I saved the house, and I saved the collection from being broken up and sold off to pay your debts. The house and the collection belong to me now, so I can protect them. You still have a home. If you don't like the arrangement, you can always leave.'

'And go where?' said Susan.

George looked uncomfortable for the first time, but his voice remained steady. 'I don't want you to go anywhere, mother. You know that.'

Bernard surged up out of his chair again, to stab a trembling finger at his entirely unconcerned son. 'I'm not senile! And I'm not weak! I can still take back control of this family, if I have to!'

He started forward. Susan grabbed hold of his arm to stop him, and Bernard threw her aside with surprising strength. She crashed to the floor, crying out sharply as she hurt herself. Bernard was too busy shouting at George to notice. Penny moved forward to help Susan. She got in Bernard's way, and he struck out at her. But I was right there, to grab his wrist in my hand and stop the blow before it reached her. Bernard swore at me and tried to pull his hand free. But he couldn't. I held him where he was, and then put some strength into my grip. Bernard's face went white as the pain hit him.

'That's enough!' said George.

It wasn't clear which of us he was talking to.

'It's all right, Ishmael,' Penny said quickly. 'I'm fine, really I am. You can let go of him now.'

I released Bernard and he staggered back, nursing his bruised wrist to his chest. Susan was back on her feet, holding herself a little stiffly from where she'd hurt herself in the fall. She shrugged off Penny's well-meaning help and went to talk soothingly to Bernard. He looked lost, confused. Susan persuaded him to sit in his chair again.

'This is why I want them here in the house,' George said quietly. 'So I can keep an eye on them. When father has his . . . moments, he doesn't remember how strong he can still be. Sometimes . . . it's hard for me to remember him the way he was before.'

'You don't have to do this on your own, Daddy,' said Chloe.

'You have your own life to lead,' said George. 'You look in as much as you can, I know that. But it's down to me. I can control him if I have to.'

'I'm not deaf,' said Bernard. 'And I'm not stupid. I know what's happening to me. Every day it feels like there's less of me . . . and I hate it.' He looked at Susan. 'I hurt you, didn't I? I'm so sorry, my dear.'

'It's all right,' said Susan. 'It's all right.'

'No it isn't,' said Bernard. And for a moment he seemed on the brink of tears.

No one wanted to say anything.

George busied himself getting fresh drinks for everyone. Conversation began again, as everyone talked about everything except what had just happened. I wondered about the possibilities of my own mental deterioration. After all, technically speaking I was older than Bernard. Physically I could go on for ages, but what about my mind? I decided I was going to have to think about that . . . and perhaps plan ahead.

'When are we going to see the mummy?' said Penny, very brightly. 'Or the rest of this marvellous collection I keep hearing so much about?'

'It's shit,' Nicholas said loudly, his voice thick with drink. 'It's all shit. I don't want anything to do with it. Never have.'

Everyone looked at him. Caroline put a staying hand on his arm, but he shrugged it off defiantly.

'When I was just a kid, I hated having to come here to visit with the grandparents. In this horrid old place.'

Susan looked at him, shocked. 'Nicky, how can you say that? You know we always went out of our way to make sure you had a good time while you were here.'

'It wasn't you,' said Nicholas. 'It was the house. And the damned collection, everywhere I looked. It gave me nightmares.'

'Where did all this come from?' said Chloe. 'You never said anything about this to me before.'

'Would you have listened, if I had?' Nicholas showed his teeth in something that wasn't really a smile. 'Daddy's little favourite.'

'Don't be horrid, Nicky,' said Chloe. 'You're drunk.'

'Doesn't make me wrong.'

'If you don't care about the mummy, why are you here now?' said Stuart.

Nicholas sneered at George. 'Because Daddy has a new wife. And so soon after Mummy died—'

He broke off, his lower lip trembling. Caroline took hold of his arm tentatively, and this time he let her. When Nicholas spoke again, his voice was cold and clear. 'A new wife could mean a new will. One that disinherits you and me, sis, in favour of the new wife and her children.'

Chloe looked at him, startled. The idea had clearly never occurred to her before, but now it had been raised . . . She looked at Stuart and then at her father. George stared at her unflinchingly, saying nothing.

She turned reluctantly back to Nicholas. 'If you really don't give a damn about the collection, why do you care who inherits it?'

'Because if it's going to be sold,' said Nicholas, 'I want my share. It's only fair I get something out of it after the way it's messed up my life.'

'I should have known,' said George, and all eyes went to him. 'It's always going to be about the money with you, isn't it, Nicky? Ever since I cut you off for threatening to talk to the museums about things that were none of their business, just to spite me.'

Nicholas smiled nastily. 'The rich and the poor have one thing in common, Daddy. Money is always going to be the most important thing in their life.'

'You're not poor!' said George.

'No,' said Nicholas. 'And I never will be while I can still make money out of this damned collection.'

59

'The family fortunes only exist to maintain the collection,' said George.

'You don't care about it, not really,' said Nicholas. 'All that matters to you is that your collection is bigger than anyone else's. That you've got something no one else has. Why couldn't you collect stamps or comic books, like normal people?'

Caroline's hand clamped down hard on his arm, interrupting him before he could say something unforgivable. Nicholas subsided, and went back to his drink.

'I suppose I've always taken the collection for granted,' said Chloe. 'Never really thought about it . . . because it was always there. I don't appreciate it, I'd be the first to admit that. I suppose it's all very fascinating if you're interested in that sort of thing . . . But I do believe it's important. Surely we can all agree on that?'

She was trying hard to be the voice of reason and bring people together. To keep peace in the family. I got the impression that had been her job for some time.

'That's why one day all of this will be yours, Chloe,' said George. He didn't even look at his son.

'But what about the will, Daddy?' said Nicholas. 'What if Marjorie gives you more children?' He grinned at Chloe. 'You really think that little gold-digger will stand by and let her precious offspring be passed over in favour of us? Better watch what you say, sis. One wrong word and you could end up out in the cold, just like me.'

60

'I'd still have Stuart,' Chloe said calmly. 'And he is all that's ever really mattered to me.'

'You say that now,' said Nicholas, 'but . . .'

'Shut up, Nicky,' said Chloe, not unkindly.

'Why are you here, Nicholas?' I said. 'If you really don't care about the collection or the mummy, and just being in the house gives you the creeps . . . Why bother turning up for the viewing?'

'Just to remind everyone I still exist,' said Nicholas. 'And that I won't be overlooked, by anyone.'

'You always were a sullen child,' said George. 'Where were you when your grandfather was throwing away the family's money? Mister big-time City banker. I tried to contact you a dozen times, but you never answered. I had to save the family on my own!'

'What makes you think it's worth saving?' said Nicholas. 'And don't say you did any of this for the family. You did it for the collection.'

Penny took it on herself to break up what was threatening to become an uncomfortable situation. She strode over to a far corner and pointedly studied an old sarcophagus standing upright on its own. The artwork and decoration were nothing special and the whole affair was rather shabby, but it had a certain presence.

'Where did this come from? It looks fascinating!'

It was a fairly obvious ploy, but everyone gratefully seized the chance to talk about something else. We all drifted over to join her. Apart from Bernard, who wouldn't budge from his chair, and Susan, who wouldn't leave him.

'Grandfather acquired this back in the fifties,' Chloe said brightly. 'There's only a dummy inside, the real mummy was destroyed long ago. Back in Victorian times there was a fad for grinding up mummies and using the powder to make patent medicines. It was all the rage.'

Penny looked shocked. 'They ground up bodies?'

'And then snorted them,' said Nicholas. 'That's your real Victorian values, right there. Destroying another country's culture just so you could shove it up your nose. Nothing changes . . .'

'Fashion can be a cruel mistress,' Caroline said vaguely.

'Empty sarcophagi have always been easy to find,' said George. 'I'm the first private collector in ages to have his own mummy.'

'And is there a curse attached to your mummy?' Penny asked, just a bit desperately.

'Of course!' said George. 'Wouldn't be a proper mummy without one. How did it go, Professor?'

'*Death shall come to any who dares remove Cleopatra from her chosen resting place,*' said Rose.

'Well, that doesn't sound at all ominous,' I said. 'Have there been any deaths attached to this mummy?'

Everyone looked at George, but he had nothing to say.

'There are stories . . .' said Stuart. 'But then there always are stories.'

'Particularly in that part of the world,' said Rose.

'Who found Cleopatra's tomb?' I said. 'I'm assuming it wasn't any officially sanctioned archaeological team. Are we talking grave-robbers?'

'Oh, tell them the damned story, Rose!' snapped George, and the professor nodded quickly.

'It is a fascinating account. Though I've been having trouble confirming some of the details. So much depends on who you talk to. It seems a group of local people all had the same dream, directing them to a particular location in the Valley of the Sorcerers. An area usually avoided because it was . . . unlucky, unhealthy. All the usual superstitions. They all ended up at the same spot, where they felt compelled to dig. And soon enough they uncovered the entrance to a tomb.

'That was as far as they were prepared to go in that place. They returned home and called for help. From people with practical knowledge of such things. Not scholars, of course, more . . . local businessmen. They excavated the tomb, and discovered a mummy with a very famous name. These people knew other people, who arranged for a quick sale and smuggled the mummy out of the country. Speed was essential, partly because it had to be done before the authorities found out . . . and partly because they'd started having bad dreams too. Now this is where it gets interesting. Within a week everyone involved in the discovery of the tomb was dead. I suppose it's always possible the smugglers killed them to ensure their silence. Such behaviour is not unknown with such people.'

'How did these people die?' I asked.

'Strangely,' said Rose. 'There were no wounds, no signs of violence, on any of the bodies. No signs of disease. They all just . . . died.'

Something in the matter of fact way he said that sent a chill down my spine. And given the way everyone else reacted, I wasn't the only one. George stirred uncomfortably.

'I don't like this talk of killing. I want to make it very clear that I don't deal with criminals. Just people with the right connections, to bypass awkward Government restrictions and get things done. It's not like I've been dealing with the Mafia!'

'Just as well,' said Nicholas. 'You might end up with a jackal's head in your bed.'

He laughed. No one else did. Caroline took his glass away from him.

'I think you've had enough for now, dear.'

Nicholas started to argue, and then stopped as Caroline looked at him. Which was interesting.

'I think it's time we got a good look at what we all came here to see,' I said.

'Of course!' said George. 'The mummy! The first Cleopatra, unknown progenitor of a famous line.'

'A long way from home,' said Stuart. 'Let's hope she's not feeling restless.'

'She's just an exhibit, dear,' said Chloe. 'And nothing happens to any part of this collection without father's permission.'

'Damn right!' said George.

And off we went, to see what there was to see.

* * *

Apart from Bernard, who still refused to budge from his chair. And Susan, who wouldn't hear of leaving her husband on his own. The rest of us, even Nicholas and Caroline, followed George through a series of dark and gloomy corridors. He kept up a stream of cheerful conversation, but it didn't make the shadows seem any less threatening. I suppose he was used to them. Everywhere we went, exotic items and curios sprang to the eye, like prizes in some disturbing fairground attraction. George strode right past them, not even looking most of the time.

Until finally we reached the room George had chosen as the setting for his special sarcophagus, with its precious contents. He took his own sweet time producing a key to unlock the door, milking the moment, and then insisted we stay out in the corridor while he went in first. To make sure everything was as it should be. We all shared amused looks at his need for drama. His mummy, his show, his way. George finally gestured grandly for the rest of us to enter. To my surprise, everyone hesitated. In the end I took the lead, with Penny quickly at my side, and we all filed in.

The first thing I noticed was that the room was packed with surveillance cameras, swivelling suspiciously this way and that, little lights glowing like beady red eyes, covering the sarcophagus from every angle. The sarcophagus stood upright and alone in the middle of the room, artistically lit by several spotlights. There were no other artefacts, nothing to detract from the main attraction. It was all very dramatic, and impressive.

The exterior of the sarcophagus was beaten gold, thickly encrusted with jewels, and the lid was a single magnificent piece of art depicting the woman within. The face was strikingly beautiful, even allowing for the usual stylization. I turned to Professor Rose.

'Why is she alone? Why has Cleopatra been separated from her regal possessions? That's not standard procedure.'

'I'm working on them,' said Rose. 'There's a lot they can tell us.'

'Aren't you afraid of triggering the curse?' I said. 'By angering Cleopatra?'

'Oh, please,' said Rose.

The sarcophagus was barely five feet tall, but it still dominated the room with its presence. A simple box, older than Christianity. We all clustered around it, studying it carefully, but none of us wanted to get too close. The heavy scents that filled the house were much stronger here. Like breathing in the past.

'What does she look like?' Penny said finally. Her voice was hushed, as though we were in church. 'The mummy, I mean.'

Everyone turned to George, expecting him to describe her with all his usual enthusiasm. But he said nothing. I turned to Rose, and then to Stuart.

'Has anyone actually seen this mummy?' I said. 'I mean actually opened the box and looked inside?'

'Not yet,' said Stuart.

Marjorie looked incredulously at George. 'You spent all that money on something you haven't even seen?'

'I've seen photographs,' said George, just as sharply. 'And I examined the paperwork very carefully to make sure everything was in order. The provenance is unimpeachable. I have dealt with these people before, and they've always proved entirely reliable. It's just that opening the sarcophagus is . . . complicated.'

'How?' I said.

'It's locked,' said Rose.

We all looked at him.

'Isn't that . . . unusual?' said Penny.

'Very,' said Stuart.

'If you haven't opened it, how can you be sure there really is a mummy in there?' said Penny.

Everyone was looking at George now. He scowled, and looked at Rose.

'I don't think the sarcophagus should be opened, just for a casual viewing,' Rose said carefully. 'Not until I've had a chance to finish my examination of the exterior.'

'Oh, come on!' said Nicholas. 'We were brought here to view the mummy. You can't fob us off with a closed box.'

'Exactly!' said Caroline. 'Viewing the mummy is what this weekend is all about.'

'I really can't recommend . . .'

'Shut up, Rose,' said George. 'My mummy, my show. Help me open the damned thing.'

Rose reluctantly produced a notebook, and he and George spent some time consulting it before attacking a complicated locking mechanism concealed on one side of the sarcophagus, holding the lid firmly in place. I moved in for a closer look, ignoring irritated glances from the other two. It was a mixture of a combination lock and the kind of sliding panels you find in Chinese puzzle boxes. Not at all what you'd expect on a coffin. Which might mean the sarcophagus wasn't what it was supposed to be, or . . .

'They locked the mummy in?' I said.

'Were they afraid she might get out?' said Penny.

'Of course not,' said George, not looking up from what he was doing.

Rose looked back at Penny disapprovingly. 'That sort of thing only happens in bad movies.'

'Or really good ones,' Penny said cheerfully.

'Why fit a lock on a coffin?' I said.

'There was a legend,' Rose said unhappily. 'Old stories which resurfaced as a result of the unusual deaths . . .'

'What kind of stories?' I asked.

'Supposedly the first Cleopatra possessed an item of great power,' Rose said reluctantly. 'Something that made her amazingly strong and extremely long-lived.'

'She still died,' said Stuart.

'Is that why they locked her inside her coffin?' said Penny. 'Because they weren't completely convinced she was dead and didn't feel like taking any chances?'

'There are many stories about the first Cleopatra,' said Rose.

I gave him a hard look. 'How can that be, when no one had heard of her before her tomb was discovered?'

'There were records inside the tomb,' said Rose. 'And old stories passed down from generation to

68

generation among the locals. Never discussed with outsiders, because no one liked to talk about them . . . Terrible warnings not to look for her tomb. And, of course, we know how that turned out.'

I was intrigued, but before I could press Rose any further George made a loud satisfied sound as the lock finally yielded to his efforts. He took hold of the heavy lid with both hands and struggled to move it to one side. Even with all his strength, he had a hard time shifting it. I moved in to help, and between us we slid it to one side, leaning it against the side of the sarcophagus. I was careful not to use my full strength in front of Stuart, just in case he had his Colonel's hat on. But he didn't seem to notice. Like everyone else, his attention was fixed on the contents of the coffin.

The mummy was there, all right. But she didn't look anything like the image on the lid. It wasn't the typical body bag and mask I'd been expecting. The body was complete, with separately wrapped torso, arms and legs. But the mummy was a shrivelled, withered thing, standing slumped against one side of the coffin. The bandages were a dirty brown, so thickly permeated with spices and preservative chemicals that I almost choked on the smell. The face was only partly wrapped, revealing a hideous distorted death mask. The eye sockets were empty, the nose was gone, and the mouth had drawn back from the teeth in an endless snarl.

'It's horrible!' said Penny.

'Imagine how you'd look after two thousand years,' said Rose.

69

'This is what the embalming process did to people,' I said. 'The Ancient Egyptians never meant their mummies to rise again. The bodies were only preserved to help support the *ka* on its journey through the afterlife.'

'That is a gross oversimplification of a very complicated belief system,' said Professor Rose.

'After two thousand years, everything we know or think we know about Ancient Egypt is never going to be more than guesswork,' I said.

'Educated guesswork,' said the professor.

We all looked at the mummy, and for a long time none of us said anything. Penny was right: it was seriously ugly. It was hard to think of anything so used up ever going for a little walk.

'You spent a ton of our money on that?' Marjorie said finally. 'This nasty piece of . . . It doesn't even look real! Put the lid back on, George. It smells.'

'Hush,' said George, still staring raptly at his prize. 'She's real. The very first Cleopatra. Show some respect! You're looking at history in the flesh.'

Rose turned abruptly to fix me with a challenging gaze. 'Well, Mister Jones? Are you ready to provide us with your expert opinion? Mister Cardavan already has mine. Let us see how closely yours agrees.'

He was jealous of his position with the family, and eager to undermine what credibility I had. Everyone looked at me expectantly. I smiled easily back at them, and nodded at the coffin's contents.

'Yes,' I said. 'That is quite definitely a mummy.

Anything more will have to wait, pending careful research into the writings on the interior of the box. You did notice those, didn't you, Professor? There will have to be chemical tests on the bandages, and X-rays to show what's inside the mummy. And so on, and so on . . . You know all this, Professor. Only fools rush in where scholars fear to tread.'

Penny applauded loudly, grinning broadly. Some of the family joined in, pleased that I'd avoided Rose's trap. He just sniffed loudly, as though I'd only confirmed his worst suspicions. I annoyed him even further by not giving a damn. Rose saw that everyone was siding with me, turned his back on all of us, and went to stand by the door. George took hold of the sarcophagus lid, and I helped him ease it back in position again.

'Isn't she magnificent?' he said quietly. 'An ancient queen of legend, right here in my home.'

'Is she everything you hoped?' I said.

'I've seen mummies,' said George. 'I knew what to expect.' He turned away, to face his family. 'Come and see what I've done with the rest of the collection! It's all very different now from how it used to be. Time for the grand tour!'

Most of us smiled indulgently, but Nicholas shook his head stubbornly.

'We've seen it. Why would we want to see it again?'

'Because I've made extensive changes in the presentation,' said George, frowning heavily. 'Something that had been neglected for far too long.'

'Like I give a damn!' said Nicholas.

71

'We are going,' said George. 'You can always go back to the drawing room and remain with your grandparents, if you want.'

Nicholas looked like he was ready to do just that, if only to defy his father and show his independence. But Caroline murmured sharply in Nicholas's ear, and he nodded reluctantly. Caroline wasn't prepared to miss out on anything. I had to wonder whether this whole inheritance issue might have started with her, rather than Nicholas. And so we moved off through the house again.

George led the way, like a man at the head of his own parade, happily pointing out items of interest and lecturing loudly on things he didn't understand nearly as well as he thought he did. Marjorie clung to his arm and did her best not to look bored. The house was a large old place, with all kinds of back corridors, hidden passageways, and rooms within rooms. Chloe and Stuart and Nicholas and Caroline just strolled along, taking it in their stride. I looked intently at everything, and Penny lapped it all up. The professor slouched along in the rear, thinking his own thoughts. The house's lighting varied from place to place, but it never really improved and the shadows remained stubbornly impenetrable.

'Would it kill you to get some proper lighting installed?' Nicholas growled.

'Too much light might fade some of the more delicate colourings,' said George. 'But mostly, I believe the proper atmosphere is important.'

The whole of the first and second floors of Cardavan House were packed with ancient

72

artefacts that had to have taken generations to accumulate. I asked George when his family first started collecting.

'It all began with my grandfather, Douglas Cardavan,' George said immediately. 'This was in the 1920s. There was a lot of interest back then in all the amazing discoveries coming out of Egypt. It became quite the done thing for those with the time and money to pay a visit to Egypt to soak up the atmosphere and see it all for themselves. If only for the bragging rights when they went home. But Douglas was never the same again.

'According to the family records he joined all kinds of expeditions, which were happy enough to take his money. He made several small but significant discoveries of his own. Could have had a perfectly respectable career . . . but it was never enough for him just to find things, he had to own them. Once it became clear he was smuggling artefacts out of the country in defiance of all the rules and regulations, no reputable archaeological team would have anything to do with him. But he didn't care. It was all about the collection and what he could get away with.'

We had now been treated to a tour of the whole of the second floor and reached the stairs leading up to the top floor. George came to a sudden halt.

'The top floor is living quarters only,' he said. 'There has always been a tacit agreement that one floor should be kept entirely free from the collection. To prevent it from overwhelming the family.' He dropped me a roguish wink. 'The women folk decided that, of course. The rest of us just go along with it for the sake of peace and quiet.'

'I've got a really nice room picked out for you and Penny, Ishmael,' said Marjorie. 'I'll show you where it is when we're done with this. It's very comfortable.'

'With rather better lighting, I hope,' said Penny.

Marjorie laughed brightly, and then stopped when no one else joined in. George cleared his throat loudly to show he wasn't done talking.

'The collecting bug became a family obsession,' he said. 'Each new head of the house took it on himself to add to the collection and expand its range.' He gestured at a wall covered with packed bookshelves. 'We've all become experts in our chosen field. Though not to your level, of course, Professor Rose.'

The tour continued. Some of the exhibits were impressive, some were valuable, and some were so obviously rare there was no way they could have left Egypt legally. I noticed that Nicholas kept hanging back and avoided looking at the collection directly. When George finally paused for breath, Nicholas suddenly started talking again.

'I hate the things with cat heads the most. They scared the crap out of me when I was small, and turned up in my nightmares for years afterwards. Cat heads on shelves and on the walls, alone and horribly alive. They looked right at me, snarling and spitting, and spoke to me in languages I didn't always understand. One of them told me I'd die here . . . in Cardavan House.'

He broke off. Caroline patted his arm

comfortingly. George sniffed loudly. His face was filled with disgust for his son's weakness. Along with anger at such an insult to his beloved collection. I decided it was time for me to change the subject.

'This is all very impressive,' I said. 'But I'm afraid I've already spotted a few definite fakes.'

Everyone looked at me. With shock and surprise. And anticipation.

'Nonsense!' said George. 'Everything here has been thoroughly checked! The professor . . .'

'Clearly hasn't finished his work yet,' I said. I pointed to a small wooden stele with barely discernible cartouches. 'Fake, I'm afraid.'

'Because it's wood?' said Rose. 'Don't show your ignorance. Clay was most usual, but wood was not unknown . . .'

'Not elm wood,' I said. 'No elm trees in Ancient Egypt.'

Rose looked at me, and then at the stele. 'You can't be sure that's elm, just from looking at it.'

'Check it yourself,' I said. 'In the meantime, take that unrolled papyrus on the wall over there . . .'

Everyone looked. Rose glared at me. 'I suppose you're about to tell us it's the wrong kind of papyrus.'

'No,' I said, 'It's a fake because whoever produced the artwork couldn't resist adding a little touch of their own. To be exact, I can see the starship *Enterprise* flying in the background.'

I pointed it out and everyone crowded forward for a closer look. The tiny starship was unmistakable once you knew what to look for. George looked thunderstruck, Rose glared at me, and Stuart nodded approvingly. Nicholas got the giggles.

'Makes you wonder what else here isn't what it's supposed to be, doesn't it?' he said happily.

'Why the *Enterprise*?' said Penny.

'Someone's idea of a signature,' I said.

'How could you see something that small in this light?' said Chloe.

'Years of experience,' I said. 'In learning to be observant.'

George stabbed an accusing finger at Rose. 'You should have seen that! What else have you missed? Maybe I should fire you and bring in Ishmael as my personal expert!'

'I hadn't reached this part of the collection yet,' Rose said flatly. 'It's a very large collection.'

'Yes,' said George, somewhat mollified. 'It is.'

Rose glared at me for a long moment. I'd made myself an enemy.

Penny decided it was time for her to change the subject. 'You started to tell us there were strange stories attached to Cleopatra. What kind of stories?'

George smiled at her, pleased at a chance to show off his learning again. And to make clear how important his new acquisition was.

'Cleopatra was supposed to be a soul thief, who killed her enemies by ripping their *ka* right out of them. She boasted she would live lifetimes sustained by the stolen life energies of others.'

'How old was she when she finally died?' I asked.

'Fifty-two,' said George. 'Doesn't sound much

by our standards, but we're talking about a period when anyone who made it past thirty was suspected of being in league with dark forces. Most died a lot younger.'

'How did Cleopatra come by these amazing powers?' said Penny. 'Did she claim to be descended from the Egyptian gods?'

'Most Pharaohs claimed that at one time or another,' said George. 'According to legend, her powers came from a magical stone that descended from the heavens. She only fell from power after the stone was taken from her.'

'Who took it?' said Penny. 'And what happened to it?'

'No one knows,' said Rose. 'It's a pity the stone didn't come with the mummy. It would make a marvellous addition to the collection.'

George let out a brief bark of laughter. 'A magical stone that could make you live forever? Damn right, Professor! I'd have given it place of honour!'

Everyone managed some kind of smile. But I couldn't help thinking that amazing things really did fall out of the sky, in my experience.

Three
Struck Down

'Well!' said George, rubbing his hands together briskly. 'On with the tour, then! Still lots to see . . .'

And then his smile disappeared, as he realized no one else shared his enthusiasm. Most of the family weren't even trying to be polite about it. There was a certain amount of glancing back and forth and shuffling of feet, as they all looked for the right way to say they'd rather suffer a horrible death than continue any further. In the end, not surprisingly, Nicholas was the first to break ranks. He stepped forward and glared pugnaciously at his father.

'I've had enough. We've admired your precious mummy and listened to your preposterous stories and made all the proper appreciative noises . . . So we can all say we've done our duty. But if I have to look at one more piece of Ancient Egyptian junk I will gouge out both my eyes and throw them on the floor and stamp on them!'

'Now, Nicky,' Caroline said quickly, 'Let's not overreact. You might have seen it all before, but I haven't . . .'

'Trust me,' said Nicholas, 'it really doesn't get any better! I'm going. You suit yourself.'

He strode out of the room and stomped off down the corridor. Caroline shot us an apologetic glance and hurried after him. Chloe was the next to step forward. She met her father's deepening scowl with a kind but determined smile.

'Sorry, Daddy, but I need to go back and see how grandfather is. He's definitely worse, compared with the last time I saw him. We may have to consider the possibility that keeping him here isn't the best thing we could be doing for him.'

'You think we should just put the old boy in a home, don't you?' said George.

'Somewhere he could get professional nursing care, yes.'

'This is where he belongs,' said George. 'Where I can keep an eye on him.'

'But is that what's best for him?' said Chloe. 'Which is why you took control of the family, isn't it? Because it was in his best interests. Come along, Stuart.'

She strode out of the room and this time it was Stuart's turn to smile apologetically, before hurrying after her. I looked thoughtfully at the empty doorway. For the first time, I'd seen some real steel in Chloe's character. She didn't strike me as someone who needed protecting. So why did Stuart want me here, really?

Professor Rose cleared his throat, and then stopped immediately when everyone turned to look at him. 'I need to go back to my room and consult my books. To do some research on that possibly unreliable stele.'

'And I can't go wandering around the house with you, George, when I should be looking after my guests,' said Marjorie. 'Besides, you know I don't appreciate the collection like you do.'

'All right then, go!' George said loudly. 'You don't need my permission! Do what you want.'

But as Marjorie followed Professor Rose out of the room I could tell how disappointed George was. He'd wanted her with him as he showed off his trophies. Even the most obsessive collectors can feel the need to have their enthusiasm validated by the approval of others. And I'd caught the look on Marjorie's face as she brushed past me. The pleasant, elegant hostess had disappeared, replaced by a woman not prepared to accept any rival in her own home. Not even a long dead one. An older man with a new young wife should have anticipated that. But George hadn't. Perhaps because he saw Marjorie as just another part of his collection . . .

Of course, I could have been reading too much into such a brief confrontation. But I didn't think so.

George smiled determinedly at Penny and me. 'So! Just us, eh? Should have known only a real expert like yourself, Ishmael, would appreciate my collection properly. Follow me. Lots to see, lots to see . . .'

He stalked out of the room and into the corridor, not even glancing back to make sure we were following. Penny and I strolled after him, taking our time. Penny moved in close, so she could murmur in my ear.

'Why are we sticking with him, darling? In order for me to be any more bored, I'd have to be twins.'

'What better way to get a complete tour of the house?' I murmured back. 'And a chance to put myself in George's good books. Just in case I feel the need to abuse that trust later. Besides, this is a good way to get to know George on his own, away from his family. To get a feel for what's going on in his head.'

'You think there's more to him than meets the eye?' said Penny.

'There would have to be,' I said.

But in the end George tired of his tour after just a few more corridors. It wasn't the same for him without a full audience to lecture and impress. He frowned more and said less, until finally we ended up back outside the mummy room. George stood before the door, thinking his own thoughts, while Penny and I waited patiently.

'I'm sure you'd like to see Cleopatra again, wouldn't you?' he said finally. 'She is the pride of my collection. My greatest prize.'

'Of course,' I said.

'Wouldn't miss it for the world,' said Penny.

'Penny loves mummies,' I said.

'I do. I really do.'

George pushed open the door and hurried in, as if he needed to reassure himself the mummy was still there. By the time Penny and I joined him, he was standing before the locked sarcophagus, rocking back and forth on his feet as he stared into the painted eyes of the face on the coffin lid. Looking at the long dead woman in a way I'd never seen him look at his wife.

'You're not going to tell me this is a fake, are you?' he said quietly.

'No,' I said. 'The sarcophagus and its contents

give every appearance of being genuine. But when it comes to those incredible stories, as to how the tomb was discovered and what happened afterwards . . .'

'Egypt is full of stories,' said George. 'Who can say what's real and what isn't, after so many years . . .'

'It's certainly an amazing find,' I said. 'But who else can you show it to, outside your family?'

'No one,' George said immediately. 'I can't trust anyone else. Doesn't matter whether it's the authorities or any of the other private collectors. They'd all want to take her away from me. Jealous, because she's mine.'

'If you can't show her off,' said Penny, 'what's the point in having her?'

'Knowing I've got her,' said George. 'And they haven't.'

Suddenly realizing he was revealing more of himself than he was comfortable with, he turned a stern look on me that made it clear the party was over.

'You've indulged me long enough, Ishmael. Don't think I'm not grateful, but I need some time to myself. You'll find the others in the dining hall.'

He gave me quick but clear directions, and then indicated the open door with a jerk of his head.

'Don't want you getting lost,' he said brusquely. 'It's a big house, after all.'

I had already memorized all the twists and turns of our journey, but I didn't mention that. I was more interested in the way his gaze kept returning to the painted face on the coffin lid, as if she was the only thing in the room that really mattered.

'If you're sure . . .' I said, but he'd already dismissed me from his thoughts.

'There's a cold meal laid out in the dining hall,' said George. 'The servants did that much before they left. You can go now.'

Penny and I had barely stepped out into the corridor before the door slammed shut behind us, and I heard the lock turn. George really wanted to be on his own.

'A boy's best friend is his mummy,' I said solemnly.

'Oh, shut up!' said Penny.

It didn't take long to get to the dining hall. I strode through the gloomy corridors, taking each turn confidently, while Penny looked uneasily around her, avoiding the deeper shadows and glaring back at the painted faces on the shelves.

'You didn't need directions. You remember the way, don't you?' she said accusingly.

'Of course.'

'You're weird, sweetie. Luckily, it's part of your charm.'

'I've always thought so.'

'Don't push your luck, darling.'

We finally ended up before a closed door at the end of another very long corridor. Rows of funerary masks stared unblinkingly from both sides, like a coldly judgemental audience. I ignored them with studied disdain, leaned in close to the door and breathed deeply.

'I can smell food. Cold meats, salads, fruit.'

'Really weird!' said Penny. 'Should we knock?'

'I don't see why.'

I opened the door, kicked it back out of the way,

and strode in as though I'd just conquered Cardavan House with steel and fire. I didn't need to look back to know Penny was shaking her head resignedly. The dining hall wasn't on the same overwhelming scale as the drawing room, but it was still a leftover from a time when the whole extended family would be expected to attend every meal. Covered by a blindingly white cloth and with highly polished candelabra set out on it at regular intervals, the dining table stretched away further than any modern family could ever be comfortable with. All the food, plates and cutlery had been arranged at the far end. A good spread – mostly regular hearty food, with a sprinkling of delicacies. And a wide choice of wines. All very civilized. The great open room was brightly lit, but completely deserted. We were the first to arrive.

'Tell me you don't find this just a bit weird,' said Penny. 'It's like the *Marie Celeste* in here.'

'The others are on their way,' I said. 'I can hear them.'

'And now annoyingly weird!' said Penny.

We made our way down the length of the table and discovered elegantly handwritten name cards to show where everyone was supposed to sit. I was tempted to rearrange them all, just for the fun of it, but the sound of approaching footsteps was too close.

Stuart and Chloe were the first to appear. They'd both changed for dinner, and surprisingly Stuart wasn't wearing his tuxedo any longer. Instead, he'd gone for a dark blue three-piece suit of impeccable style and respectable dullness. At first, I thought he'd only done it so he could show off his old-school tie. Stuart might not have enjoyed his schooldays, but he wasn't above taking advantage of them. And then I smiled inwardly, as it occurred to me that he'd probably hired his tuxedo for the weekend and didn't want to risk getting food stains on it.

Chloe was all dressed up in an elegant evening gown of emerald green with gold piping, and a single string of pearls. She looked like she belonged in a room like this, at a meal like this. Stuart stood proudly at her side. They made a handsome couple.

They went straight to their places without checking the name cards. Stuart pulled back Chloe's chair for her, but she stopped him with a gesture. She smiled charmingly at me, and I gave her an equally meaningless smile in return. Like two boxers touching gloves in the ring before the fight begins.

'So!' Chloe said brightly. 'What work, exactly, do you and Stuart have in common, Ishmael?'

'Sorry,' I said. 'What I do is always going to be confidential. You should understand that, Chloe, working for Black Heir.'

She cocked her head slightly to one side, as though to see me more clearly. 'There's always something in your voice when you say Black Heir . . . As though you don't exactly approve of us. Why is that, Ishmael?'

'I had good reasons to leave,' I said. 'And if you work for them long enough, you'll find good reasons too.'

'The work we do is important,' said Chloe. 'We keep people safe.'

'Black Heir are scavengers and bullies,' I said flatly. 'In it for the profit. Protecting people is just a side line.'

'Do you know something about Black Heir that I don't?'

'More likely, you know something you haven't allowed yourself to think about properly.'

'I looked you up in Black Heir's records when Stuart said you'd be coming,' said Chloe. 'I couldn't find your name anywhere. But then Ishmael Jones doesn't sound like a real name, anyway.'

'It suits me,' I said.

'What if I looked for your face?'

'You wouldn't find anything,' I said. 'Black Heir holds its own secrets closest of all.'

Stuart was starting to look uncomfortable. Perhaps fortunately, we were interrupted by Bernard and Susan's arrival. The old man was wearing a formal tuxedo that looked like it had seen a lot of hard use, though it still retained its basic elegance. Susan wore an evening gown whose style hadn't been fashionable in ages, presumably because she felt comfortable in it. She'd put on a few diamonds here and there for the occasion.

'Food!' Bernard said loudly, looking approvingly at the fare spread out before him. 'Good. As you get older food becomes more important, because it's all you've got left.' He smiled at Susan. 'Apart from you, of course.'

Susan smiled happily, relieved at his good temper.

Professor Rose drifted in, tightly buttoned up in a suit that didn't suit him. It was obviously his idea of what formal wear should be, from a man who wasn't used to wearing such things. I couldn't resist teasing him a little.

'Has your research revealed anything useful, Professor, about the two fakes I pointed out?'

'The papyrus is obviously a forgery,' he said brusquely. 'The stele requires further examination.'

He sat down stiffly in the place assigned to him, and gave all his attention to the ranks of cutlery around his plate so he could avoid further conversation. I let him do so.

Nicholas and Caroline made what she obviously intended as a grand entrance. With her arm linked firmly through his, the better to control him, they posed for a moment in the doorway so everyone could properly admire them. Nicholas wore his tuxedo with sullen indifference, while Caroline wore a scarlet evening gown of obvious expense, carefully cut to show off her figure to its best advantage.

'Oh, how marvellous!' she said, beaming at the food on the table rather than her fellow guests. 'Now this is truly splendid, isn't it, Nicky? Exactly what you'd expect at a grand old country house. I always say no one does hospitality like the country set. Pity there's no staff to wait on our every whim, but then you can't have everything.'

Nicholas just grunted, looking like he wished he was somewhere else. He headed for the table, dragging Caroline along with him.

And finally, Marjorie made her appearance. Given that she'd been so keen to leave her husband to look after her guests it was a little odd that she was the last to arrive, but her new look explained everything. She'd changed into a shimmering sparkling number that clung to her magnificent figure, and had put on a whole new set of jewellery that gleamed and glistened at every point. She'd even taken the time to change her hairstyle and redo her make-up. Marjorie had no intention of being upstaged by her husband's collection. She wanted to remind him why he'd chosen her in the first place, and that a dead queen was no match for a young wife. She smiled brightly on one and all as she burst in like a ship under full sail, only to stop abruptly as she realized that her intended audience wasn't there.

'Where's George? Why isn't he here? Oh, this is just typical of the man!'

Bernard looked pointedly at me and Penny. 'Should we hold the meal? So the two of you can go upstairs and change?'

I cut in quickly, before Penny could say anything. 'No thank you,' I said. 'We don't really do formal. And besides, we're too hungry to wait. Isn't that right, darling?'

Penny gave me a frosty smile, but nodded quickly. 'Absolutely, darling. Positively starving.'

We all sat down and reached for the silk napkins in their silver holders. I wasn't actually hungry, I just wanted an opportunity to quietly interrogate the others about George in his absence.

Penny leaned in close. 'You know very well I have a wonderful new evening dress in my luggage that would have stunned everyone. You just didn't want to carry all our suitcases up to the top floor!'

'Hush,' I said. 'I'm working.'

We all helped ourselves to food, passing the

88

Willow Pattern china back and forth. Everyone piled up their plates, apart from Nicholas, whose thoughts seemed to be elsewhere. Caroline frowned as she saw how little he'd taken and took it on herself to load his plate with some of everything, presumably on the principle that since it was free they might as well make the most of it. Stuart opened the wine with practised ease, and we each had a little something for our good health. Everyone tucked into their food with a good appetite, apart from Nicholas, who just pushed his food around with his fork. Before I could even start my subtle questioning, Caroline took it upon herself to fill the quiet with her usual aggressively friendly chatter.

'What a marvellous old house this is! I always thought I would do well in a setting like this. So sophisticated! And a fascinating collection, of course. I never knew anything about it until Nicky told me all about it after we were married. And I thought . . . I have to see that!'

Given the way Nicholas stabbed viciously at his food at that point, I was pretty sure coming back to Cardavan House had been Caroline's idea, so they could stake a claim for his inheritance. Caroline struck me as the kind of woman who wouldn't give up on anything valuable she thought she had a claim to.

She chattered on, but no one was listening. Marjorie ate quickly but neatly, keeping an eye on everyone to make sure we realized how much trouble she'd been to on our behalf. Bernard concentrated on his food, while Susan concentrated on him. Professor Rose ate steadily, with more concentration than enjoyment. Stuart and Chloe exchanged glances.

'Why did you come back to the old family house, Nicholas?' asked Stuart. 'After so long away?'

'Though we are of course glad to see you, Nicky,' Chloe said quickly.

'You, possibly,' said Nicholas. He smiled coldly round the table. 'I came back to see the mummy and the new wife. Father's latest acquisitions. Caroline pointed out to me how important they both were in the current scheme of things.'

'I'm delighted you're all here,' said Marjorie, smiling implacably. 'This is the first time I've had the whole family gathered together under my roof. I'm looking forward to getting to know everyone.'

'Are you?' said Nicholas. 'Are you really?'

'Nicky . . .' Chloe said warningly.

Nicholas ignored her, his cold smile fixed on Marjorie. 'Tell me . . . How long were you my father's secretary before you decided you wanted to be more than that?'

'I was there when he needed me,' said Marjorie, entirely unmoved by his tone. 'Where were you when your mother died? George was in pieces, and we couldn't find you anywhere.'

'We did try, Nicky,' said Chloe. 'But you weren't answering your phone, and no one knew where you were.'

'Business,' said Nicholas. 'I was busy.'

'Your father knew he could always depend on me,' said Marjorie, complacently.

There was a long pause, while everyone thought their own thoughts. It was just threatening to become awkward when Professor Rose suddenly turned to fix me with a cold stare.

'Have you ever actually been to Egypt, Mister Jones? In your capacity as an expert on all things Egyptian?'

I wondered if he'd heard anything the rest of us said, or if he'd been spending all his time working out the best line of attack.

'I know Egypt,' I said.

'And what did you do there?'

'On my last visit, I was part of a team investigating a newly discovered secret chamber deep within the Great Pyramid of Giza. Waste of time, in the end.'

'Was that when you were with Black Heir?' said Chloe.

'No,' I said. 'I was with someone else then.'

'And you're not going to tell us who.'

'Our world is full of secrets,' I said. 'Usually with good cause.'

Stuart was starting to look really uncomfortable. He would have liked to shoot Chloe a warning glance to tell her not to discuss such things in front of civilians, but her attention was fixed on me. I smiled easily back at her, as though we were just chatting. I was used to dealing with awkward questions, and awkward questioners.

'How did you and Stuart meet, originally?' said Chloe.

I looked at him. 'Do you want to take that one, Stuart?'

'Sorry, my dear,' Stuart said gruffly. 'That's still classified. I can't talk about some aspects of my work, any more than you can.'

'But I thought you'd left all that behind, dear,' said Chloe.

'I have,' said Stuart. 'Mostly.'

She gave him a stern 'We'll talk about this later!' look.

'I'm really not following your drift,' said Caroline, frowning prettily. 'What's Black Heir?'

'A security firm,' I said. 'Nicholas did tell you that George does security work?'

'Oh, yes! Of course! He tells me everything.'

And then Caroline gave Nicholas a stern 'We'll talk about this later!' look. He ignored her, intent on the food he wasn't eating.

The conversation limped along, not really going anywhere. I managed a few carefully phrased questions about George and his work, but no one seemed to know anything. Which was, after all, as it should be. And then, suddenly, Marjorie looked at the oversized clock on the wall and frowned.

'Where is George? He should have joined us by now. Of course, it's not unusual for him to be late. He always says punctuality is for underlings. And he can get caught up in his collection, especially when he's got something new to obsess over . . . Sometimes I have to send the servants to remind him it's time to eat. But this is a bit much . . . even for him. Excuse me.'

Stuart and I exchanged looks, as Marjorie produced her mobile phone and punched angrily at the numbers.

'George always has his phone with him,' she said, not looking up. 'Because he never knows when he might get an important business call. It's ringing . . .'

92

We all waited, watching anger give way to worry in Marjorie's face. She turned her phone off and looked at us numbly. 'It's gone to voice mail.'

'Father doesn't normally like to miss a chance to play host,' said Chloe.

'He was disappointed that we wouldn't continue with his tour,' said Stuart. 'He could be spending extra quality time with his mummy, just to make sure we realize how important she is.'

'Yeah . . .' said Nicholas, pouring himself another glass of wine. 'That sounds like father. His collection always was more important to him than his family.'

'Not now, Nicky!' said Chloe. She turned to Stuart. 'He should have been here by now.'

'Do you want me to go and remind him?' said Stuart. 'He might not take too kindly to that.'

'Serve him right for worrying us,' said Chloe.

'I want George here!' said Marjorie. Her voice was rising, becoming shrill. 'Someone needs to go and drag him away from that damned mummy. This is my first big family occasion and I won't have it ruined!'

I nodded to Stuart, and he nodded back. We rose to our feet.

'We'll go,' I said. 'You all carry on with your meal. He's probably just lost track of time.'

'Then why isn't he answering his phone?' said Chloe.

'Probably turned it off so he wouldn't be bothered,' said Stuart. 'Wouldn't be the first time he's done that.'

There was general nodding around the table. People began to relax a little. Even Marjorie

93

seemed a little happier now someone was doing something. Penny caught my eye and raised an eyebrow. I shook my head slightly and looked quickly round the table. She got the point. I needed her here to keep an eye on everyone.

'Him and his damned mummy!' said Nicholas. 'He always did have more time for the dead than the living.'

'Oh, shut up, Nicky!' said Caroline.

I hurried through the gloomy corridors with Stuart at my side. He'd started out in the lead, but quickly become uncertain. He might be a frequent visitor to Cardavan House, but it was still a really big place.

'How can you remember the route so well?' he said. 'You only came this way once.'

'I have an infallible sense of direction.'

'Inside a strange house?'

I shot him a brief smile. 'That's where most of my work is, these days.'

There wasn't a sound to be heard in the corridors, and nothing moved anywhere. Cardavan House felt like a ghost town. Cat faces and jackal heads stared coldly as we passed. I had to fight an impulse to snatch them off their shelves and throw them around, just to put them in their place.

'You think something's happened to George, don't you?' said Stuart.

'Don't you?'

'But do you have any reason to believe something's happened?'

'I haven't seen or heard anything,' I said carefully. 'I came here to ask a few questions and perhaps indulge in a little light burglary. Did you have any reason to believe something serious was going on here?'

'I hope George is all right,' said Stuart. Not answering my question.

When we finally got to the mummy room the door was closed. I tried the handle, but it wouldn't open. I turned to Stuart.

'He must have locked himself in with his mummy after Penny and I left him.'

'He could have started back,' said Stuart.

'We would have passed him on the way,' I said.

Stuart banged on the door with his fist, taking out his frustration on the heavy wood. 'George, it's Stuart. Come on, man, it's time for dinner! Everyone's waiting, and Marjorie's in a real strop.'

We waited, but there was no response. I put my face right next to the door. I couldn't hear any movement inside, but even past the rich heavy scents of the house I could make out the flat coppery smell of freshly spilled blood. I couldn't tell Stuart that, so I just straightened up and frowned.

'I have a bad feeling about this. Who else would have a key?'

'Only George,' said Stuart. 'The mummy was his special prize.'

'I say we break the door down and apologize later,' I said.

Stuart nodded curtly. 'Do it.'

I put my shoulder to the door. Normally I could have slammed it off its hinges with one good effort, but I didn't want to do that in front of Stuart. So I took three attempts before I gave it a real hit. The door slammed open, and I hurried in with Stuart right behind me. And there was George, lying on the floor before the sarcophagus, in a pool of his own blood. Someone had smashed his head in. The coffin had been opened. The lid lay on the floor some distance away, and the mummy was gone.

'Go stand by the door,' I told Stuart. He didn't move, his gaze fixed on George. 'Stand by the door, Colonel!'

He tore his gaze away to look at me angrily. 'Why?'

'There's nothing we can do for George,' I said. 'He's dead. So now we have to do our job. And that means not compromising the crime scene any more than we have to. I need you to keep a watch on the corridor and make sure we're not interrupted.'

He nodded stiffly. 'You are sure he's dead . . .?'

'Look at him,' I said. 'The whole side of his head has been caved in.'

Stuart put up a hand to stop me. 'I can see that.'

'You're not used to bodies, are you?' I said, not unkindly. 'You normally have people to deal with this sort of thing for you.'

'I was in the army,' Stuart said harshly. 'I've seen action, and my fair share of death. But it's different when it's family. Poor George, poor Chloe . . .'

'Go watch the corridor,' I said. 'I know what to do.'

He went to stand in the doorway. I moved forward, stepping carefully over and around the blood. There was a lot of it, pooled around the body and spattered across the floor. There was even arterial spray across the inside of the open sarcophagus, indicating that George was standing before it when he was attacked. His face had been reduced to a pulp. George hadn't died quickly or easily. Someone had put a lot of effort into doing this much damage.

I leant over the body for a closer look. No defensive wounds. Which suggested George had been struck down from behind while his attention was fixed on the mummy. Except . . . George had locked the door after Penny and I left. A quick look around confirmed there were no windows, and no other exits. I thought about it. George could have unlocked the door for someone he didn't consider a threat . . . And then I straightened up and looked inside the sarcophagus again as something caught my eye.

'What is it?' asked Stuart, turning round immediately. 'What do you see?'

'There's blood all over the inside of the coffin,' I said. 'There are no gaps, no voids. So the lid was off when George was attacked, and the mummy wasn't there.'

'Are you suggesting . . .?'

'I'm not suggesting anything,' I said. 'I'm just following the evidence to see where it leads. George could have unlocked the lid to better admire his prize and then been struck down from behind, so someone could steal the mummy. But perhaps George didn't stay down. Maybe he fought the thief and was killed . . . No. No, there aren't any bloody footprints or scuff marks on the floor to support that. What the hell happened here?'

'The mummy could have unlocked the lid from

inside,' Stuart said steadily. 'Come forth and struck down the man who had her brought so far from her resting place. Remember the curse? *Death shall come . . .*'

I looked at him. 'You really believe that? You honestly think a shrivelled-up two-thousand-year-old body killed a man and is currently wandering around the house?'

'It doesn't seem very likely, does it?' said Stuart.

'No,' I said. 'It doesn't.'

'George can't have been dead long,' said Stuart. 'It's been barely an hour since we were all in here with him. Who was the last to see him alive?'

'The murderer, obviously,' I said. 'Otherwise, Penny and me. And George was still alive when we left.' I looked again at the blood on the floor. 'Whoever did this must have ended up soaked in George's blood. But of course everyone changed their clothes for dinner . . .'

'You think it was one of the family?'

I looked at him. 'There's no one else in the house. Apart from Professor Rose.'

'Penny and you were the only ones who didn't change for dinner,' said Stuart, 'so it couldn't have been you.'

'Well spotted,' I said. 'Even from the short time I've been here, I can identify any number of motives. Everything from money to hurt feelings. Professor Rose would seem to have less motive than most: with George dead he'd probably lose his special access to the collection.' I broke off to look thoughtfully at Stuart. 'You had your suspicions about George. Did you come here to confront him, and things just got out of hand?'

'I was with Chloe from the moment we left this room,' Stuart said steadily. 'I never left her side for a moment.'

'I believe you,' I said. 'If only because it complicates things unutterably if I don't.' I looked back at the body. 'Whoever did this couldn't have done it with bare hands. He or she must have used the proverbial blunt instrument. And brought it into the room, since there was nothing like that in here. Which speaks to planning and preparation. And . . . this would have taken a lot of strength. It's hard work to bash someone's head in.'

'You'd know,' said Stuart.

'Yes,' I said. 'I would.'

'More than human strength?' said Stuart. 'From some ancient corpse infuriated at having its tomb desecrated and its rest disturbed?'

'Will you stop that! You saw the state of the thing. That mummy couldn't have killed George even if the killer had used it as a blunt instrument.'

'Are you sure?' said Stuart. 'I've seen things . . .'

'So have I,' I said. 'And yes, I am sure.'

I moved around the perimeter of the room, checking the walls for sliding panels or hidden doors. I even studied the floor and ceiling carefully, looking for trapdoors, but I couldn't find anything. I went back to the sarcophagus.

'The lock that held the coffin lid in place hasn't been forced or broken,' I said. 'So either George unlocked it or the killer knew how to open a very complicated locking mechanism. The only other person who knew that was Professor Rose.'

'It could have been opened from the inside.'

'No, it couldn't.' A thought struck me. 'The door was still locked when we got here . . .'

Stuart nodded quickly. He checked the keyhole, inside and out. 'No key.'

I knelt down beside the body and searched through George's pockets. I soon found the key I'd seen him use earlier. I put it in my pocket and got to my feet again. Stuart came forward to join me, frowning.

'If he still had the key – the only key – how did the killer get out?'

'I hate locked-room murder mysteries,' I said.

Someone screamed. We both looked round quickly. Nicholas and Caroline had got tired of waiting. They were standing together in the open doorway, staring in horror at the dead body. Caroline's face was white with shock. She clapped both hands over her mouth to keep herself from screaming again and turned away from the body, burying her face in Nicholas's chest. He held her almost absently, his wide eyes fixed on the dead man. A mixture of emotions showed in his face, but he looked more confused than anything. I heard more feet approaching. Caroline's scream had got everyone's attention.

Marjorie arrived, pushed Nicholas and Caroline out of her way, and then howled miserably as she saw what had happened to her husband. Penny was quickly there to take Marjorie firmly by the shoulders and turn her away. Marjorie collapsed into Penny's arms, and Penny made quiet soothing noises as Marjorie sobbed wildly.

100

Part of me wondered whether the grieving young widow might be overdoing it just a bit.

Chloe was the next to arrive. Nicholas and Caroline had retreated into the corridor and Chloe stood framed in the doorway. Her face went slack with shock and she trembled violently. Stuart was quickly there to comfort her. She let him hold her, but her eyes didn't leave her dead father. She wasn't crying.

Professor Rose turned up next, breathing hard from exertion. He took one look at the body and turned away quickly, one hand pressed to his mouth to keep from vomiting.

Finally, Bernard and Susan arrived. He looked even more confused than usual, but somehow he found the strength to comfort his distraught wife. It was getting crowded around the door. I looked at Stuart, and he used all his natural authority to gather everyone up and usher them out into the corridor. Marjorie didn't want to go. Penny had to physically manhandle her out of the door with Chloe and Stuart's help. I followed them out into the corridor and pulled the door shut. Marjorie glared at me through tear-filled eyes.

'Why aren't you doing something to help George? Help him!'

'I'm sorry, Marjorie,' said Stuart. 'George is dead. There's nothing we can do.'

'What are you saying?' Marjorie said fiercely. 'He can't be dead! How can he be dead?' And then she stopped, and laughed shrilly. 'The sarcophagus was open! You all saw! It killed him . . . His precious mummy killed him! I told George that awful thing would be the death of him!'

'More likely someone stole it,' I said. 'The thief didn't expect anyone to be here, and George was killed in the struggle.'

'Then the thief could still be here in the house!' said Rose.

'Don't even think of going after the killer,' I said. 'That goes for all of you.'

'Why not?' said Marjorie. 'Do you want him to get away?'

'He could be armed,' I said.

'We have to call the police,' said Chloe.

'And the security people,' said Stuart.

A thought struck me. I opened the door and looked quickly round the room. 'The security cameras aren't working.' I looked back at Stuart. 'How is that possible?'

'It shouldn't be,' he said immediately. 'Unless . . . the whole system has been shut down.'

'Who could do that?' said Penny.

'Anyone who knew the correct password,' said Stuart. 'Only George was supposed to know, but he could have told someone else.'

'If all the cameras are down,' I said, 'no one outside the house knows anything has happened. There's no record of the murder, and no one is coming to help.'

'I'll have to contact the security people,' said Stuart. 'Tell them what's happened. But it will still take them a good hour to get here.'

'This is why you should never place your faith in electronic systems,' I said.

'Not a good time to gloat, sweetie,' Penny murmured.

'Who are you, really?' said Chloe, glaring at

me accusingly. 'That dead body didn't bother you at all.'

'Ishmael is a security expert,' said Stuart. 'I brought him in to check how secure the house really was.'

'I should have known,' said Chloe. 'And you should have told me, Stuart!'

'I knew he wasn't a real Egyptian expert,' said Rose.

'Stop talking!' said Marjorie. 'Stop just . . . talking! Call the police!'

'Given George's business, there are security issues,' said Stuart. 'We let the security people in first and call the police afterwards.'

Chloe nodded, reluctantly.

'I want the police!' said Marjorie.

'We're in the middle of nowhere,' Chloe said sharply. 'The security people will get here quicker. Call them, Stuart.'

'Let's all go back to the drawing room,' said Stuart. 'I'll make the call, and Ishmael can get on with his work.'

It took him a while to persuade everyone, but eventually they all left. Only Penny remained with me.

'I knew it!' she said. 'A family gathering in a dark old house and a mummy with a curse on it . . . Someone was bound to be murdered! Seeing that this isn't an official case, Ishmael, we could just leave and let the security people handle it.'

'No,' I said. 'This happened while I was here. I feel responsible.'

'Of course you do,' said Penny. 'That's so you. Sweet, but at the same time infuriating!'

103

'Besides,' I said, 'aren't you curious?'

'A dead body and a missing mummy?' said Penny. 'Of course!'

We went back into the room. Penny looked at the dead man and pulled a face. 'Can't we at least . . . cover him up?'

'What with?' I said. 'There's nothing here, and I'm not giving up my jacket.'

'But he looks . . . really bad.'

'Then don't look at him.'

'Does it make me a bad person,' said Penny, not allowing herself to look away, 'that I don't feel so bad about this because I didn't like George much?'

'No,' I said. 'Just means you're human. Fortunately, I'm not so limited.'

'Stop patting yourself on the back before you strain your arm,' said Penny. She took a deep breath and turned to me. 'How's your bloodhound nose? Are you picking up any signs of another presence in the room? A particular perfume or aftershave, or body odour?'

'All I'm getting is blood,' I said. 'This house is so full of smells that they're covering up everything else. Look at the blood, Penny. Not a single footprint. Which means our killer stepped carefully around it when leaving. Even though the manner of the murder suggests a frenzied attack, it was followed by a carefully unhurried exit.'

'So our killer was a professional?' said Penny.

'Or a sociopath,' I said.

'Or a mummy?'

'Don't you start. Let's just say the killer was

104

definitely a monster.' I knelt down beside the body again. 'Looks to me like the beating went on even after George was dead. The skull isn't just cracked, it's been smashed right in. That would take a lot of strength.'

'More than human?' said Penny.

'Stop it . . . And the features are so disfigured from repeated blows it's easier to identify George by his clothes than his face.'

'Hold everything!' Penny said excitedly. 'Are we sure this really is George?'

I had to smile. 'You think the murderer took the time to dress someone else in George's blood-stained clothes, then leave with George's body and the mummy? You've been watching too many *Midsomer Murders*. No, this close I can recognize George's scent. It's him.'

'Oh, ick!' said Penny. 'Still, whoever did this must have been covered in George's blood.'

'I know,' I said. 'But everyone changed for dinner. Convenient . . .'

'Could someone have planned that?' said Penny. 'Waited till George was on his own and everyone else was getting changed, and then struck? So it would be possible to put on new clothes without raising any suspicions?'

'Could be,' I said. 'We'll search everyone's rooms for bloodstained clothing, but it's almost certainly been disposed of by now.'

I went to look at the sarcophagus again. 'Someone opened the lock, and only George and Professor Rose knew how to do that.'

'But the professor had it all written down in his notebook,' said Penny. 'Anyone could have read it . . . Besides, can you see Rose doing this kind of damage? He's a bit weedy.'

'You'd be surprised what people can do when they're mad enough,' I said.

'Ishmael, I know you don't want it to be the mummy . . . But why not? We've seen stranger things. Hell, you are a stranger thing.'

'But not supernatural,' I said. 'Far more likely the mummy was stolen. It was the most valuable thing in the house.'

'But what about the curse?'

'What about it? The stories told of people in Egypt dying suddenly from no obvious cause, with no signs of violence. Not like this.'

'All right. Perhaps the theft was planned but the murder was accidental? If George hadn't been here . . .'

'The killer has to be one of the family,' I said. 'Who else would have been in a position to learn the password to shut down the security? And they'd have known George was likely to still be in here. He was obsessed with his new acquisition.'

'Any one of them could have a good reason to steal the mummy,' said Penny, reluctantly. 'Nicholas and Caroline talk about money all the time, because George cut Nicholas off. Chloe might have been worried about being cut out of the will. Maybe Marjorie wasn't getting on as well with George as she liked to make out. And Bernard and Susan might have been afraid of being evicted. Hold it! Why didn't the thief take the sarcophagus as well? I mean, it's gold. It must be worth a fortune in itself.'

'And it weighs a ton,' I said. 'It took George and me just to move the lid.'

We both looked round sharply as Stuart appeared in the doorway.

'I can't stay long. The family are going crazy, and Chloe is in a hell of a state. I've phoned the security people. They say all communication between them and Cardavan House was cut off forty-seven minutes ago. None of the cameras spotted anything untoward before then, though they're going through the recordings just in case. Because the proper password was used, they assumed George had a good reason for shutting everything down. Apparently he's done it before, when he wanted some privacy.'

'Are they on their way?' said Penny.

'I told them to hold off for the time being,' Stuart said steadily. 'They'll come when I call them, but I don't want them getting involved until we know what's going on. We still don't know what George may have done to acquire the mummy. We need to be sure of the facts before we start official proceedings. So I can protect Chloe.'

'We need the security people here to protect the whole family from a thief and a murderer!' said Penny.

'All the surveillance systems in the grounds are still working,' said Stuart. 'Entirely separate systems. Security are adamant no one has entered the grounds since you two arrived.'

He didn't sound at all happy about that. No doubt wondering which member of his adopted family might have killed another member. No wonder he wanted it to be the mummy.

'We could still be looking at a professional thief,' I said. 'Someone who knew how to avoid the security systems, inside and out. It could be done. I could do it.'

'Probably not a good time to be pointing that out, sweetie,' murmured Penny.

'You saw the grounds,' said Stuart. 'Acres and acres of nothing. There's nowhere for anyone to hide. It has to be one of us.'

'And that has to include you, Colonel,' I thought, though I didn't say it. 'Maybe the only way you could protect your wife was by sacrificing her father and removing the evidence of what he'd done.' It didn't seem likely, but people have done less for worse reasons. Stuart's only alibi was his wife's word that they were together all the time, and if she was as protective of him as he was of her . . .

'I still say we shouldn't rule out the mummy,' Penny said stubbornly. 'I mean, it is gone.'

'It's just a dead thing wrapped in bandages,' I said. 'What happened here suggests human rage and human motivation.'

Stuart moved slowly forward and looked down at the body. 'I'm sorry, George. Whatever you might have done, this isn't how I wanted it to end.' He looked at me accusingly. 'I brought you here to prevent something like this happening!'

'If you'd wanted me to act as a bodyguard, you should have said. The best I can do now is find out who did this.' I looked at him steadily. 'Are you sure that's what you want, Colonel? For me to follow the evidence, wherever it leads?'

'Yes,' said Stuart. 'Whoever it leads to.'

Four
There is No Thief

We made our way quickly back to the drawing room, keeping a watchful eye on every closed door and sudden side turning. The heavy hush seemed to swallow up the sound of our footsteps. It felt like walking through the depths of a forest at midnight while some predator watched from the darkest part of the woods. There was no walking mummy. I knew that, I just wasn't sure I believed it.

I had no trouble remembering every twist and turn of the way. Penny was used to that, Stuart wasn't. He watched me as much as our surroundings, as though hoping to pick up some clue that might explain me to him.

'Do you really think there might be a professional thief somewhere in the house?' Penny said finally. I think as much for the comfort of hearing her own voice as anything.

'It's possible,' I said. Being diplomatic, because Stuart was there.

'Is it?' he said. 'God knows I want there to be a thief! Otherwise it means one of my family is a murderer. But it doesn't seem likely.'

'Look on the bright side,' I said. 'It could be Professor Rose.'

Stuart shook his head. 'He's harmless. All he cares about is his work. He's spent all his time here immersed in the collection. For him, people are just something that gets in the way of more important things.'

'Many predators take on a harmless aspect,' I said, 'until it's time for them to strike.'

'Oh, very deep!' said Penny.

'I thought so,' I said.

'You really reckon Rose could be the killer?' said Penny. 'I'm having a hard time seeing someone his size beating a man as big as George to death, even with a whole bunch of blunt instruments.'

'I haven't enough evidence to accuse anyone yet,' I said. 'It's just that Rose is the only outsider. As far as I can tell, everything was fine here until he arrived.'

'Everything was fine until that damned mummy arrived!' said Stuart. 'Maybe that's its curse – the power to change everything for the worse just by being here.'

He broke off as I stopped suddenly and looked sharply around me. Stuart and Penny stared quickly up and down the corridor. It was all very still, very quiet. The corridor was empty, all the doors were closed. And although the shadows seemed more than usually deep and dark, none of them were moving.

'What is it, Ishmael?' Penny said quietly. 'Did you hear something? I can't hear anything.'

'I'm not sure,' I said. 'It's just . . . something doesn't feel right.'

'Listen for the beat of the cloth-wrapped feet . . .' said Penny.

Stuart looked at her. 'What?'

'Old mummy movie reference,' I said. 'And no, that's very definitely not what I'm hearing.'

'Well, what are you hearing?' said Stuart.

'Nothing,' I said. 'It's more like . . . a feeling. Of being watched by some unknown presence. Like an alarm just went off inside me that I didn't even know was there.'

'What are you talking about?' said Stuart.

'Beats the hell out of me,' I said.

'Then I think we should get moving,' said Stuart. 'It feels to me like we're in enemy territory, in a really good place to be ambushed.'

'Are you armed, Colonel?' I asked.

'No. Didn't think I'd need a weapon among my own family. I brought you here to investigate a security breach, not a murder.'

'Ishmael?' said Penny. 'Is there something here?'

'There is something . . .' I said. 'But I don't think it's here.'

I set off again at a brisk pace, and the others had to hurry to keep up with me.

I didn't see or hear anything untoward all the way back to the drawing room. Until I finally approached the door at the end of the corridor and heard raised voices arguing. As we drew closer, Penny and Stuart picked up on them too. I walked right up to the door, slammed it open, and barged in with Penny and Stuart right behind me. Everyone in the room stopped shouting at each other and glared at me. Some of them looked angry, some looked upset. But no one looked guilty.

111

'You didn't even think to lock the door in our absence?' I said.

'Father had the only set of keys to the house,' said Chloe. 'Unless you've got them now. You searched his pockets?'

'All I found on him was the key to the mummy room,' I said.

'So where are the other keys, if George didn't have them?' said Stuart.

'He might have had them on him when he was attacked,' I said.

'And the killer has them now?' said Penny.

'Not necessarily,' said Stuart. He turned to Marjorie, standing on her own by the fireplace. 'Where did George put the house keys when he wasn't carrying them?'

'I don't know!' said Marjorie. 'George always took care of things like that. We didn't bother much with locks except at night. We are miles from anywhere, after all, and surrounded by security . . .'

'Did he ever give the keys to anyone?' I said.

'No,' Marjorie said immediately. 'They were his keys. He wouldn't trust anyone else with them.' She looked at me uncertainly. 'What's going on?'

'I don't know yet,' I said.

I was more intrigued that the young widow had stopped weeping and didn't even seem particularly distraught any more. I looked round the room. Bernard was back sitting in his chair, scowling hard as though pursuing a thought he couldn't quite grasp. Rubbing his hands together as though they were cold. Susan had pulled her chair up beside him, so she could comfort him with her presence. She patted his arm now and again, but he didn't react.

Chloe didn't look like she'd been crying over her father's death, but then she'd never struck me as the crying kind. She came forward to join Stuart, and he reached out and took both her hands in his. They smiled at each other as though they were the only ones in the room. I wasn't sure which of them was being strong for the other. Maybe they both were. Nicholas and Caroline stood together, presenting a united front to the world, as always. Nicholas had a large glass of something in his hand, and looked more sullen and aggrieved than anything else. As if George's death was just another in a long series of annoyances, designed to make his life even more difficult. Caroline murmured urgently in his ear, as though prompting him, and he nodded quickly and raised his voice.

'Caroline and I think we should leave. Right now.'

'Well you can't,' said Chloe. 'We're all part of a murder investigation.'

'Are you saying we're suspects?' said Caroline, her voice rising sharply. With anger, I noted, rather than dismay.

'Everyone here is a suspect,' said Stuart. 'Don't take it personally.'

'Everyone here is in danger!' said Caroline. 'As long as we stay in this horrible old house. You really think you can stop us if we decide to walk out of here and drive off?'

'I can call the security people and have them

arrest you the moment you leave the grounds. And of course they're not police, they're not required to be polite.'

Nicholas smiled sourly at him. 'Once a soldier, always a soldier, eh Stuart? You just love to be in charge and bark orders, don't you? No wonder you married Chloe. You're just like the rest of this family. Bullies, one and all.'

'Quiet, Nicky,' said Chloe. 'Grown-ups talking.'

Caroline gripped her husband by the arm. 'He's just one man. Are you going to let him talk to you like that?'

Nicholas shrugged. Whatever decisiveness Caroline had instilled in him was gone. He smiled at her, just a little sadly. 'Given that Mister Ex-military there looks like he could wrestle both of us to the floor before we even get to the door, I'm going to let him say whatever he likes. You wanted me to ask what there was to stop us leaving. Now we know. We're not going anywhere, dear. Would you like me to get you a drink? I'm having another one.'

'You've had enough.'

'Not yet I haven't.'

'We have to keep our heads clear, Nicky,' said Chloe, not unkindly. 'We have to figure out what's happening here.'

'That's your job, sis,' said Nicholas, as he drifted over to the bar. 'Let me know if you come up with anything particularly impressive, so I can applaud.'

'What are you all talking about?' Bernard said loudly. Surprisingly, his gaze was clear and his mouth firm. As though discussion of his son's

114

death had roused him from his usual half-life. He fixed me with a sharp, penetrating gaze. 'You. You look like you know what you're about. What are the facts?'

I ran through what I was sure of. It didn't take long. Everyone listened carefully, and when I finally finished they all looked at each other. The general reaction in the room seemed to be a reluctant resignation. As though now I'd spelled out the facts of George's death they had no choice but to accept it. Chloe was the first to pull herself together. She fixed me with a challenging look.

'What do you think happened? Who killed my father?'

'We don't know yet,' said Stuart.

'What's the matter, Mister Jones?' said Chloe, not taking her gaze off me for a moment. 'Can't you speak for yourself?'

'Some things are clear,' I said. 'Whoever attacked your father must have got blood all over his clothes.'

'And we all changed for dinner,' said Chloe, immediately getting the point.

Everyone started to speak at once, saying they hadn't seen any blood on anyone's clothes and quickly vouching for their partner. Apart from Professor Rose. He sat quietly to one side, saying nothing, his hands neatly arranged in his lap. He'd been so quiet for so long everyone had forgotten about him. He watched us all with placid, disinterested eyes. He had no one to vouch for him, and he knew it, but he didn't seem at all troubled. The family quickly ran out of indignant protestations as they realized I wasn't paying

115

them any attention, and then they turned to look at Rose as he stood up and stared calmly about him.

'Since there is no one to speak for me, I must speak for myself. I swear to you, on my reputation as a scholar, that I am no killer. You are welcome to search my room for bloodstained clothing. I can assure you, you won't find any.'

No one seemed too impressed by that. I could see suspicion growing in everyone's face. Until Chloe spoke up again, addressing me.

'You said my father was killed by a blunt instrument, but there wasn't one in the mummy room.'

'That's right,' I said.

'Then the weapon must be hidden in the house, somewhere,' said Chloe. 'We have to find it.'

'Why, dear?' said Susan. 'What does it matter? Your father is dead, do we have to talk about this?'

'Yes, grandmother, we do,' said Chloe. 'There might be evidence on the weapon that could tell us who the killer is.'

'We'll find it,' said Stuart. 'But that will mean searching the whole house, top to bottom. Nowhere can be considered off-limits. Does anyone have any objection to their room being searched?'

Nicholas snorted briefly. He was already well into his second drink. 'Would it do any good if we did?'

'Shut up, Nicky,' said Chloe. 'You're drunk.'

'No I'm not,' said Nicky. 'But I'm working on it.'

116

Caroline put a hand on his arm. 'Please, Nicky. Don't. I can't do this on my own.'

He looked at her for a moment, and then put his glass down on a side table. 'All right, dear. Just for you.'

I looked round the room. No one liked the idea of someone rummaging through their belongings, but they couldn't come up with a good enough reason to say no.

'A full search of the house,' Nicholas said thoughtfully. 'Does that include father's study?'

'Of course,' said Stuart.

'Well, I hate to sound mercenary, but I'm going to,' said Nicholas. 'Does anyone know where father's will is? Does anyone know what it says? And if it's been altered in any way recently?'

He looked meaningfully at Marjorie. She stared defiantly back at him.

'He was talking about updating his will. So it's probably still with his London solicitors.'

'Did he change his will recently?' Chloe asked, frowning.

'No,' said Marjorie, smiling brightly and just a bit triumphantly. 'George changed his will right after we were married. In my favour. He said he wanted to make sure I would be properly looked after if anything were to happen.'

'What sort of changes did he make?' said Chloe, but Marjorie just smiled at her.

'Told you, sis,' said Nicholas. 'Looks like we're screwed, after all.'

'If there's been foul play, that means we can contest the will,' said Caroline, glaring daggers at Marjorie. 'And you can bet your fake tits we will.'

'Well said, my dear,' said Nicholas. 'It's not the principle of the thing, it's the money.'

Chloe rounded on him. 'Our father is dead, Nicky! Doesn't that mean anything to you?'

'Yes,' said Nicholas. He met her gaze squarely, and his voice was suddenly cold and bitter. 'It means I'm free of the old monster at last. Free of his loud voice and his hard hands. Of the disgust he never bothered to hide, at a son who never wanted to be anything like his father. He's dead now, so let's hold a celebration! He can't hurt us any more.'

'You do realize that sounded very much like a motive for murder?' Stuart said carefully.

Nicholas shrugged. 'I've never made any secret of how I felt about him, but if I'd wanted to kill him I'd have done it long ago. I didn't want him dead. Not before I'd proved to him I could make a life for myself that had nothing to do with him.'

'But you still came back to make a claim for your inheritance . . .' said Stuart.

'Caroline insisted,' said Nicholas.

'We seem to be wandering away from what's really important,' said Rose. 'What is going to happen to the Cardavan collection?'

We all looked at him.

'You think that's what really matters?' said Chloe.

'Of course,' said Rose. 'Oh . . . I see. Don't expect any crocodile tears from me. I never cared for the man, and he never cared for me. We were just useful to each other. The Cardavan collection is far more important than one man's death.'

'But the most important part of the collection

has just been stolen,' I said. 'So who, in your expert opinion, would be the most likely buyer?'

'An interesting question,' said Rose. 'The mummy should go to a museum, of course, where her history and provenance could be properly established. But I suppose there's no denying a private collector would pay more. And a museum might find itself under pressure to return the mummy to Egypt, for political reasons. If she really is who she's supposed to be, of course.'

'Is there some doubt?' said Penny.

'All the paperwork I was shown supported everything that was said about her,' Rose said carefully. 'But papers can be forged, and people can be fooled. Especially when they want to be. George allowed me unrestricted access to every other part of his collection, but I was only ever allowed to see the mummy when he was there. I never got to examine her. I want her to be the first Cleopatra because of everything that would mean . . . but as a scholar I must have hard evidence before I can commit myself.'

'What about the curse?' Bernard said suddenly. He stared defiantly at everyone from his chair. 'No one's talking about it but we're all thinking of it, aren't we? *Death shall come* . . . and all that. I remember the fuss made over the curse of Tutankhamun. My father told me all kinds of stories about that. Now my son is dead and the mummy is missing. Do you really expect me to believe some thief could have got in here past all our surveillance systems? Hah! I oversaw the installing of most of those systems, and there isn't a thief in this world good enough to get into

Cardavan House without tripping all kinds of alarms. It's actually easier for me to believe in a two-thousand-year-old mummy coming to life . . .'

'What a horrid thought!' said Susan. 'It could be hiding anywhere, just waiting for another chance to kill again . . .'

'Hush, hush old girl,' said Bernard. 'Don't upset yourself. We're just talking, that's all. We're perfectly safe here. And help is on its way.'

I glanced at Stuart, but he avoided my gaze. Because we both knew no one was coming. Chloe intercepted the gaze, and glared at both of us because she didn't understand it. Chloe struck me as someone who didn't like it when people kept things from her. Which was ironic, considering that was her job with Black Heir. I wondered how long Stuart would be able to keep quiet before Chloe browbeat the truth out of him.

'Are we safe here?' she said loudly. 'Really? I don't believe in criminal-mastermind thieves, any more than I believe in reanimated mummies. Do I have to be the one to say it? Someone in this room killed my father!'

There was a long pause, but no one seemed particularly surprised or shocked at the idea.

'Any idea who?' Nicholas murmured. 'Only I might want to shake his hand and maybe pin a medal on him.'

'Not now, Nicky,' said Caroline.

'You feel the same way I do.'

'And yet you were ever so upset when we found the body,' said Penny.

'Of course I was upset,' Caroline said defiantly.

120

'Seeing him . . . like that. But let's be fair. I barely knew the man, and what I did know I didn't like.'

'Even though you were all over him earlier?' said Chloe.

Caroline smiled back at her coolly. 'We all do what we have to, to get what's rightfully ours.' She looked at Nicholas. 'Especially when the man you love doesn't know how to be strong because he's had it beaten out of him by his father. It doesn't matter, Nicky, I can be strong enough for both of us.'

'But if you found out that your husband had been excluded from George's will?' I said.

'You can stop right there,' said Caroline. 'I couldn't have killed George because that wouldn't have got me what I wanted. I needed him alive so I could work on him, persuade him to my way of seeing things. To reinstate Nicky.'

'She would have done it, too,' said Nicky. 'Caroline can be very persuasive.'

'I'll bet,' said Chloe.

'She's a very dominant personality,' said Nicholas. 'And you love it,' said Caroline. They smiled at each other fondly.

Chloe cleared her throat loudly to bring everyone's attention back to her. She fixed me with a challenging gaze.

'You and Stuart keep bringing up father's security work, but I don't see what that has to do with how he died. Unless you know something you're not telling the rest of us.'

'Isn't that your job?' I said.

'Don't push your luck,' said Chloe.

121

'Sorry,' I said. 'That's part of my job description.'

'We have to find Cleopatra and return her to her sarcophagus,' said Rose. As though nothing any of us had said was of any importance. 'If she is who she's supposed to be, she is an important part of Ancient Egyptian history. She can't be allowed to disappear. Or be damaged. And if there is a curse . . . the sooner she's put back where she belongs, the better. We must search the house and find her.'

'What if she doesn't want to be found?' said Penny.

'Stop it . . .' I said.

'What if she defends herself?' said Penny, pressing on regardless. 'If she's already killed once . . .'

'Am I going to have to make you breathe into a paper bag?' I said. 'Look, in the unlikely event of my having to go head to head and toe to toe with a shrivelled-up two-thousand-year-old thing, I think I can probably take her.'

'But can you find her?' said Chloe.

'Finding things is also part of my job description,' I said. 'Doing something about them pretty much covers the rest.'

'Ishmael really is good at tracking things down,' said Penny. 'He's part bloodhound. Though you probably don't want to know which part.'

'Who exactly do you work for, Ishmael Jones?' said Chloe.

'Someone who works for Black Heir should know better than to ask questions like that,' I said.

'I vouch for him,' said Stuart. 'That should be enough.'

Chloe gave him a hard look, and he met it unflinchingly.

'It occurs to me,' said Rose, in a voice entirely untroubled by all the things the rest of us had been discussing, 'that if the thief is still in the house he might be helping himself to other treasures from the Cardavan collection. There are many items of considerable value small enough to be carried away easily.'

That got the family's attention. Death and its mysteries were one thing; losing part of their inheritance was quite another.

'Give me a list, Professor,' I said. 'Of descriptions and locations, and I'll see if anything's missing.'

'They're scattered all over the house,' said Rose. 'I shall have to come with you to point them out.'

'Damn your precious bits and pieces!' Susan said loudly. She was the only one in the room who still seemed on the edge of tears. 'My son is dead! All that matters is finding his killer.'

'With the interior cameras down, we have no way of tracking him,' said Stuart. 'He could be anywhere.'

'Can't Security turn the cameras back on,' said Penny, 'now they know what's happened?'

'Apparently not,' said Stuart. 'Or at least not without the proper reactivation password. Someone is sticking to the letter of the agreement after falling down on the job once.' He looked at Marjorie. 'I don't suppose there's any chance you know?'

'Haven't a clue,' said Marjorie. 'George always took care of everything like that.'

'Didn't he trust you?' said Penny.

'George didn't trust anyone,' said Marjorie. 'And yet somebody was still able to get to him.'

She didn't appear too upset about that, more thoughtful. Stuart looked round the room, but if anyone knew the password they were keeping it to themselves.

I took Stuart to one side, so we could talk quietly together. 'I'm going to have to search every room in the house. For the thief, and the mummy. I also have to look for bloodstained clothing, a possible murder weapon, and missing items from the collection. That could take a while.'

'It might be quicker if I went with you,' said Stuart. 'Someone needs to guard your back.'

'Thanks for the thought,' I said. 'But I work better with Penny. And I need you here, to talk to these people. Because you're family, they might open up to you where they wouldn't to me. Talk to them, listen to them. But don't let any of them leave this room. The last thing we need is them scattering in all directions.'

'Very well,' said Stuart. 'You tear the house apart, I'll keep the family together.' He glanced covertly round the room. 'Given that the killer could be in this room, I'm not sure which of us is going to be in the most danger.'

'It's usually me,' I said. 'But I'm used to it.'

I went back to Penny. 'Fancy a little excursion round the house, and a chance to poke your nose into other people's private business?'

She grinned broadly, and bounced on to her feet. 'You know me so well! Let's go make a mess, strip people's secrets bare, and see what there is to see.'

'You're still hoping it's the mummy, aren't you?' I said.

'Of course! If only to see the look on your face.'

'Not going to happen,' I said.

I raised my voice, and everyone turned to look at me. I told them what Penny and I were going to do. It didn't go down well, but apparently none of them felt in a position to object.

'I take it we can rely on your discretion where private things are concerned?' said Caroline.

'Almost certainly,' I said.

'This is just an excuse for you to snoop,' said Chloe.

'I don't need excuses,' I said.

'Do what you have to, boy,' said Bernard, and Susan nodded.

'Please don't break anything,' said Rose.

Marjorie just looked at me.

Chloe turned to Stuart. 'Why aren't you going with him? Who put him in charge?'

'I did,' said Stuart. 'I trust him to get the job done, and so should you.'

'When all this is over, we are going to have a long talk,' said Chloe.

'Looking forward to it immensely, my dear,' said Stuart.

Penny bounced out of the door and into the hall, humming a merry tune, while I gave the room one last 'Behave yourselves!' look before going after her. The moment I shut the door behind me, I heard the sound of heavy furniture being dragged into place to form a barricade. Penny smiled sweetly.

'*Déjà vu* all over again. So many of our cases seem to involve people barricading themselves inside rooms against unknown enemies. Even though it rarely works out as well as you'd expect. So, how are we going to start this search?'

'Room by room,' I said. 'And then floor by floor.'

'This is going to take a while,' said Penny.

There were lots of rooms and lots of potential hiding places, and we had to look in all of them. I didn't even try to be neat, just tossed things around as necessary and moved on. I didn't see or hear anything to suggest we weren't alone, but it still felt like someone or something was watching us. I spent the most time in George's study, because I'd promised Stuart. The locks on the door and George's old-fashioned desk drawers were no match for my strength. I leafed quickly through piles of paperwork, but couldn't find anything useful. The wall safe, hidden behind a particularly obnoxious piece of modern art, opened easily to my experienced hands. But all it held was valuables.

No household keys, no written-down pass-words, and absolutely nothing about the mummy. And no computers, not even the most basic laptop. I had to wonder whether someone might have got there before me.

I searched every room on the ground floor, with

Penny's gleeful help, and turned up nothing of any use. I ran a quick eye over the various shelves and display cases, but nothing seemed to be missing. At least, I didn't spot any gaps. And still no sight or sound of a thief or the mummy. The house was full of a heavy, suffocating silence, along with the constant fog of ancient and modern stinks. But what bothered me most was the silence. Cardavan House didn't seem like somewhere people lived. It was a place for dead things. And for people more interested in death than life.

Upstairs on the second floor we encountered more of the same. Everywhere we went something from the collection would catch my eye, as though it was keeping watch on us. I was already tired of gold and silver, cat faces and jackal heads, and endless bits of pottery; remnants of a time so long past we couldn't really be sure what they were remnants of. Room after room, with never any trace to show the living had left their mark.

And yet I kept stopping suddenly to glare at the unmoving shadows. Not because I saw or heard anything, but because a strange new inner alarm kept going off, as though it was desperately trying to warn me of some real and imminent danger. Like some last-ditch defence mechanism that I'd never needed before. Penny waited patiently every time we stopped, but it was clear from the expression on her face that she had no idea what was bothering me. And I couldn't explain, because I didn't understand either.

We made it to the third floor – the family's living quarters – and Cardavan House finally felt like someone's home. No more shelves or display cases, no sarcophagi or unrolled papyrus; just a deep-pile carpet, pleasant wallpaper and flowers in vases. The scents on the air were fainter and far easier to take, but silence still hung over everything like a shroud. I stopped at the top of the stairs to peer down the long landing.

'You know,' said Penny. 'We should really have brought our suitcases up from the hall.'

'I am not going back down for them,' I said. 'You can, if you want.'

We made our way down the corridor, kicking in doors and rooting through each room's contents. The first few were empty. The beds were made up and there were fresh flowers in vases, but the air had a flat dusty smell that suggested only occasional use. The first occupied room turned out to be Nicholas and Caroline's. Easy enough to tell: their earlier clothing was still lying strewn across the bed and the floor from when they'd changed in a hurry for dinner. I checked it all carefully, but couldn't find a single blood spot.

Two suitcases stood below the window, both securely locked. I broke the locks and rummaged cheerfully through the contents, with Penny peering over my shoulder. More clothes, and the usual travelling odds and ends. Most of it surprisingly cheap and basic . . . not quite what you'd expect from someone who claimed to be a success in the city.

'If they're seriously short of money,' I said, 'and if George made it clear he had no intention of changing his will back in their favour . . .'

'Whoever beat George's head in was really mad at him,' said Penny. 'Hello! What's that?'

'That' was a pair of padded handcuffs, a ball gag, and something that made me wince just to look at it.

'Nicholas said his wife had a dominant personality,' Penny said solemnly.

'No wonder she wanted reassurances about our discretion,' I said.

The next room was Stuart and Chloe's. The tuxedo he'd started out in was still hanging on the front of the wardrobe. Not a speck of blood on it. There were signs the two of them stayed there on a regular basis: toiletries set out on the dressing-table, family photos showing familiar faces grouped together, all of them smiling gamely. I checked the wardrobe. Chloe had almost as many changes of clothes as Penny. But there were no bloodstains.

The door to the next room was locked. I put my shoulder to the heavy wood and the door jumped open. The room appeared to be unoccupied, until I noticed the single suitcase standing at the foot of the bed. It wasn't locked. Books, papers and learned journals filled the case. Professor Rose had brought his own library with him. But although he had to have been staying in this room for some time, he'd made no impression on it. When I opened the wardrobe, it contained four sets of exactly the same clothes. Just like the ones he was wearing earlier. No bloodstains on any of them.

'Why are they all the same?' said Penny.

'Old scientist's trick,' I said. 'Einstein's idea.

So you don't have to waste time every day deciding what to wear.'

'Scientists are weird,' said Penny. 'However . . .'

I knew what she meant. If there were four similar suits, why not five? The fifth having been carefully disposed of because it was covered in blood.

We finally reached two sets of connecting rooms facing each other at the end of the corridor, both large enough to form comfortable suites. George and Marjorie's suite was extremely comfortable, with every conceivable luxury. It was all very neat and tidy, and when I checked the wardrobe the clothes were entirely free of incriminating bloodstains. Again, lots of family photos. But no photos anywhere of George with his previous wife.

Bernard and Susan's rooms were large, comfortable and well furnished. But to be restricted to just a few rooms after so many years of having the run of the house . . . Everywhere I looked there were old-fashioned items, reminders of times past. Lots of photos in silver frames, showing the family at different times. And one photo of Bernard and Susan on their wedding day. They looked so young, so full of hope; with no notion of how their lives were going to turn out. Everything about their rooms had the feeling of old people living in the past, because that was where they felt most at home.

Penny and I went back on to the landing. There was nowhere else to go, we'd run out of rooms. No bloodstained clothes, no murder weapon, and no sign anywhere of a thief or a perambulating mummy.

'What now?' said Penny. 'Check the walls for sliding panels or hidden doors?'

'Someone would have said something if there were any,' I said. 'I've been keeping my eyes open, but there's none of the usual signs. All that's left is to go back down and start the interrogation. Because if there is no thief and no wandering mummy . . .'

'Then one of them must be the killer,' said Penny. 'That was always going to be the most likely bet.'

'It's sad, when a girl has to give up her illusions,' I said.

'I will slap you, and it will hurt.'

'Save it for Nicholas.'

Back down three flights of stairs, back through the corridors, and nothing broke the silence of the house apart from the heavy slap of our shoes on the wooden floors. But I still kept a careful watch on our surroundings. Eventually I knocked politely on the drawing room door. There was a pause, and then a cautious voice made itself known.

'Who is it?'

'Who do you think?' I said. 'A thief wouldn't knock, and a mummy wouldn't need to. Let us in and we'll tell you what we found.'

'You mean what we didn't find,' said Penny.

'Let's not confuse the issue,' I said.

There was the sound of furniture being dragged back. Then the door opened just wide enough for me and Penny to squeeze through, before it was shut again. Everyone in the room stared at us expectantly, apart from Stuart, who was pushing a heavy table back against the door.

'You know,' I said, 'you could simply wedge a chair under the door handle. That would do the job just as well.'

Stuart straightened up and gave me a cold look. 'You might have mentioned that before you left.'

'What did you find?' said Chloe, cutting across him.

'Nothing,' I said. 'No sign of any intruder, no evidence, and nothing unusual.'

I carefully didn't look at Nicholas or Caroline as I said that last bit.

'But the mummy must be somewhere!' said Rose. 'And did you find there were any other items missing from the collection?'

'The mummy appears to have been very carefully hidden,' I said. 'I didn't spot anything else missing.'

Rose sniffed loudly. 'Knew I should have gone with you.'

'You can't have looked properly,' said Bernard, thumping the arm of his chair with his fist. 'The thief must be somewhere. He has to be found! No one steals from the Cardavans and gets away with it!' He stopped, as he realized we were all looking at him. 'What?'

Susan looked at him disbelievingly. 'Our son is dead, Bernard!'

He looked confused for a moment, as though he'd lost track of the conversation, and then shook his head. 'Yes, yes, I know that. Of course I know that, I'm just saying . . .'

His voice trailed away. He looked lost. Susan patted his arm. She looked like she'd like to grieve but couldn't find the time.

Stuart jammed a chair under the door handle, with rather more emphasis than was called for, and came back to join the rest of us. He stood at parade rest, with his hands tucked behind his back, and gave everyone the same hard look.

'If there is no thief, then the killer has to be one of us. Someone in this room killed George.'

They all looked at each other, while I looked at them. No one liked the idea, but none of them spoke out against it. There was even a sense of relief in the room that someone had said what they were all thinking. Professor Rose raised one hand tentatively, like a child at school.

'I do have an alternative explanation as to what may be happening here . . .'

'Really?' I said. 'Do tell, Professor.'

'We have to consider the curse,' Rose said carefully. 'I don't normally give credence to such ideas, but there is a long tradition of Ancient Egyptian curses striking down those who fail to treat Egypt and its treasures with proper respect.'

'George respected the hell out of that mummy!' said Marjorie. 'He couldn't keep away from it!'

'But the manner of the tomb's discovery and the way in which Cleopatra was brought here show anything but respect,' said Rose. 'Let us not forget all those people who died in Egypt for daring to disturb Cleopatra's rest . . .'

'What about the dreams that led the local people to the tomb?' I said, just to be contrary. 'Doesn't that argue someone wanted the tomb found?'

'But who sent those dreams?' said Rose.

'I don't believe in curses,' I said flatly. 'Or mummies who walk.'

133

'Then why couldn't you find the mummy?' said Rose.

'Excuse me,' said Penny. 'But if this mummy was powerful enough to come out of her coffin and kill George, why would she feel the need to hide?'

'Who knows why the dead do what they do?' said Rose.

'You really believe this?' said Chloe.

The professor suddenly looked old and tired. 'I don't know what to believe any more. But I think . . . we have to face up to the possibility that this could be the Cardavan family's past catching up with it. All those years of looting and pillaging for their own satisfaction. All the precious things smuggled out of Egypt and brought here, so the Cardavans could gloat over them in private . . .'

'I have to ask, Marjorie,' said Stuart. 'How was George able to raise enough money to pay for such an expensive prize?'

And finally, there it was. The big question out in the open at last. Marjorie just shrugged.

'I know he acquired the mummy illegally. That's hardly a shock to anyone here, is it? But I never knew any of the details, I just knew it was very expensive. He wouldn't tell me how much because he knew I wouldn't approve. Not when that kind of money would have been better spent maintaining this crumbling old house. But he couldn't resist dropping hints. He said the mummy was the most important item his family had ever acquired. A personal triumph, he said. But you all saw what was in that box. A nasty smelly thing . . .'

She glared at Rose. 'Well, the collection's mine now. And I don't want any of it! It's all going. Your stinking collection killed my husband!'

'Did you know the mummy was brought here illegally, Professor?' I said.

'I suspected as much,' said Rose. 'All the paper-work I saw was perfectly in order, but I never really believed it. Because there was no way the Egyptian Government would ever have agreed to such an important find leaving their country. I knew it was wrong but I never challenged George, because if I had he might have cut off my access to the collection. But now I have to wonder . . . If I had said something, if I had made a fuss and insisted the mummy be turned over to a reputable museum, would George be alive now?'

'It had to catch up with us eventually . . .' said Chloe. 'I still won't accept the idea of a living mummy, but once they found out what had happened could the Egyptian Government have sent special agents to seize Cleopatra and make an example out of the man who'd finally gone too far?'

'Chloe!' said Susan. 'This is your father you're talking about!'

'Yes,' said Chloe. 'But there was a thief in this house, after all.'

'Egyptian secret agents?' said Rose. 'I suppose if they were angry enough . . .'

'Security are adamant no one entered the grounds,' said Stuart.

'But if they were professionals . . .' said Chloe.

'No,' Stuart said flatly. 'It's just not possible.

I know you want the killer to be an outsider, Chloe, but it has to be one of us.'

'I need to check out the collection,' Rose said stubbornly. 'I can't help feeling it holds the answer to everything that's happened here. And no one knows the Cardavan collection like I do.'

'It's dangerous out there,' I said.

'You said you couldn't find any trace of the thief or the mummy,' said Rose. 'So who is there to be afraid of out there?'

'He doesn't want you running off, Professor,' said Nicholas. 'After all, you might be the murderer.'

'Nicky!' said Chloe.

'Hey, it's not like he's one of us,' said Nicholas. 'Come on! What do we know about the professor, really? The only man in this house more obsessed with the collection than father. If he did make a fuss over the mummy and father fired him . . .'

Everyone looked at Rose. He stared back, all calm defiance. 'I am a scholar, not a man of violence. You're right, the collection is all I've ever cared about. So I will now go and make sure it's still intact. I have to do something, and this is something only I can do.'

'All right!' said Stuart. 'Go and check. If only so we can rule out the idea of a thief. But you can't go on your own.'

'None of you trust me,' said Rose. 'So why should I trust any of you to guard my back?'

'I'll go with you,' said Stuart.

Rose nodded slowly. 'Given that you're an ex-military man, I suppose I'd feel safer with you than with any of the others.'

'Then let's go,' said Stuart.

'You don't have to do this, Stuart,' said Chloe. 'It could still be dangerous out there.'

'I have to make sure he's safe,' said Stuart.

'And that I don't run?' said Rose.

'That too,' said Stuart.

He pulled the chair away from the door. Rose strode past him and out into the corridor without looking back at any of us. Stuart went after him and closed the door. I stepped forward to wedge the chair back in place.

'Leave that chair where it is!' Caroline said loudly. 'If they can leave, so can we!' She glared round the room, defiantly. 'Let's be honest, none of us feel safe here. If one of us is a killer . . . Oh, don't look at me like that, Nicky! I never liked these people. I saw what they did to you. Come on, we're going.'

'Where can we go?' said Nicky. 'You know Stuart will stop us long before we can get to our car.'

'He's busy, right now,' said Caroline.

'I'm not,' said Chloe.

'Screw you, you snotty cow!' said Caroline. 'You really think you can stop me?'

'Yes,' said Chloe. 'And Ishmael probably could, too.'

Caroline looked back and forth between us, and didn't like what she saw. She was still searching for something to say when Bernard suddenly rose from his chair. Susan quickly joined him. Bernard glared at me. 'I'm taking Susan up to our rooms. So I can barricade the doors and wait for Security to get here. Since we can't be sure who's who and what's what, it's the only sensible thing to do.'

I decided I'd better compromise, before things got really out of hand.

'All right!' I said. 'If you don't feel safe in this room, I'm not going to force you to stay here. No one can leave the house, but you should be safe enough in your own rooms. As long as you don't go wandering off, for any reason.'

'What if we need to go to the loo?' said Caroline. 'There aren't any *en suite* bathrooms in this dump, remember?'

'I think you'll find there's something under the bed in a house this old,' I said. 'A chamber pot, for emergencies.'

'Oh, ick!' said Penny.

'Let's go, Nicky,' said Caroline.

'Wait till everyone's ready,' I said. 'Then you can all go up together. It'll be safer that way.'

'I'd like to see anyone get in my way!' said Caroline. She strode over to the fireplace, grabbed a heavy poker and brandished it at the room.

'My son was struck down with a blunt instrument, wasn't he?' said Bernard.

We all looked at the poker, including Caroline.

'There's no blood on it,' she said. 'Come on, Nicky.'

'Yes, dear.'

They left together. Caroline leading the way.

'Are you sure there's no one else in the house?' said Chloe.

'I didn't see anyone,' I said.

'Are you armed?'

'No. I don't carry weapons.'

138

'Then what use are you as a security man?' said Marjorie. 'How can you protect us?'

'You're safer with him than anyone else,' said Penny. 'Trust him. I do.'

Marjorie sniffed. 'Yes, well you would say that, wouldn't you?'

Just for a moment, Penny looked at me. And I knew she was remembering how many of her family died at Belcourt Manor before I stopped the killer. I saved her; but couldn't save anyone else. The moment passed, and Penny looked steadily at Marjorie.

'He saved my life, when no one else could.'

We all jumped as the door burst open. I'd never got around to putting the chair back in place. I braced myself, but it was only Stuart. He looked very upset.

'What is it?' said Chloe. 'Where's Professor Rose? Has something happened?'

'I lost him!' Stuart said grimly. 'We were walking down a corridor . . . I turned a corner and suddenly Rose wasn't with me any more. I went back to look for him, but there was no sign of him anywhere.'

'Could someone have sneaked up behind you?' I said. 'Grabbed Rose and dragged him away?'

'I was a soldier!' said Stuart. 'And spent over a year in Afghanistan. I would have heard something. No, I think he deliberately gave me the slip.'

'I don't understand,' said Marjorie. 'Why would he go off on his own?'

'Because he didn't trust me after all,' said Stuart.

'You think he's making a run for it?' said Penny.

'No,' said Stuart. 'He knows about the outside surveillance. I think he just wanted to check out his precious collection without me around.'

Chloe moved forward to talk quietly and soothingly to her husband. Telling him it wasn't his fault. I had to wonder if Stuart could have done away with Rose for reasons of his own, and then returned with this somewhat unlikely story. But why would he do that? He had no motive. Unless Stuart saw Rose as a threat to Chloe . . .

'The professor just wants to loot the best of the collection for himself, while he can,' said Marjorie.

'No, that's what you'd do', I thought but didn't say.

'The exterior cameras will catch the professor if he's dumb enough to leave the house,' said Stuart. He broke off and looked around. 'Where are Nicholas and Caroline?'

'Gone up to their rooms,' I said.

'And you didn't try to stop them?' said Stuart.

'They were pretty determined,' I said. 'Or at least Caroline was. Short of knocking them down and sitting on them . . .'

'And don't think we didn't consider it,' said Penny.

Stuart let out a brief bark of laughter. I liked him rather better for that.

'I am not staying here!' Bernard said loudly. 'I don't like it here. I'm taking Susan up to our rooms.' He scowled at me. 'Unless you think you can knock me down, boy?'

Susan put a calming hand on Bernard's arm,

but he shrugged it off roughly. She didn't say anything. She looked like she was used to it. She glanced apologetically round the room.

'He'll be better, upstairs. Among his own things. He'll calm down there, once I've got him settled.'

'Don't talk about me like I'm not here, woman!' said Bernard.

'All right!' said Stuart. 'Go if you must!'

I realized Stuart felt seriously restricted in what he could say or do in this house, among his adopted family. That's why he'd brought me in.

'I really wanted it to be a thief,' Susan said quietly. 'You know where you are with a thief. Let's go, dear.'

Bernard smiled briefly. 'Don't you worry, old girl. I don't need anyone's help to protect you.'

'Ishmael is good at his job,' said Stuart.

'Is he?' said Bernard. 'Everything was fine here until he turned up. Come on, Susan, you stick with me.'

'If those two are going to their rooms, so am I,' said Marjorie. 'If only for a little peace and quiet, away from the rest of you.'

'I'll walk up with you,' said Chloe. 'And then hole up in my room.'

'I'd rather Stuart went with me,' said Marjorie.

'I'm sure you would,' said Chloe. 'But my husband has work to do.'

She shared a smile with Stuart, and then led the others out of the room. Once they were gone, Stuart shut the door carefully and looked at Penny and me.

'Have you got anything you couldn't discuss

in front of the others? Something in our line of work?'

'I've got nothing,' I said. 'No evidence of anything out of this world. Just a feeling . . . that there's something wrong with this house.'

'Oh, everyone who comes here feels that way,' said Stuart. 'I blame the collection.'

'You honestly think the professor deliberately disappeared on you?' said Penny.

'That's what it felt like,' said Stuart. 'I think he wanted to do something that he didn't want the rest of us to know about.'

'What do you know about Professor Rose, Colonel?' said Penny. 'I'm assuming you used your official connections to dig into his background?'

'Of course,' said Stuart. 'No one gets close to my family without my knowing all about them.' He smiled briefly at me. 'Well, usually . . . Rose is just what he appears to be. A respected historical expert, with a solid body of published work in his chosen field. Not much of a life outside his work, but then that's scholars for you. I don't see him as the killer . . . I see him as a victim in waiting. Even more so, now I'm not there to protect him. I should never have taken my eyes off him . . .'

'None of this is your fault,' I said.

'George went out of his way to welcome me into the family after I married Chloe,' said Stuart. 'He wasn't an easy man to get along with, but then few people are who are worth knowing. I would have been ready to throw him to the wolves to protect Chloe, but I did everything I could to protect him. Nevertheless, he died. And I can't let anyone else be hurt.'

He left the room. To be with Chloe.

'I've never understood family loyalties,' I said.

'Of course you can't,' said Penny.

'Because I'm an orphan?'

'Because there's no one else like you.' She stopped as a thought struck her. 'Have you ever come across another alien passing as human?'

'I've worked on a lot of cases with alien connections,' I said. 'First with Black Heir, and later with the Organization. But I've never met anyone like me.'

'How can you be sure?' said Penny. 'If they were as good at hiding their true nature as you are . . .'

'I suppose it would depend on how badly they needed to stay hidden,' I said.

'Would you like to meet others like you?' said Penny.

'Only if they were like me,' I said.

Five

The Wrong Kind of Footsteps

'Is there anywhere in the house we haven't looked?' said Penny. 'We checked out the kitchen, the bathrooms, the cupboards and closets . . . What about the cellar or the attic?'

'There isn't an attic,' I said. 'I checked the ceiling on the third floor. No access point. Same goes for a cellar. No way down. We've been everywhere and seen everything.'

'Then why couldn't we find the mummy?' demanded Penny. 'I mean, it has to be somewhere . . .'

'I'm giving the matter some serious thought,' I said.

'Do you think it might be avoiding us?' said Penny. 'Watching from the shadows, sneaking around behind us, hiding in places we've already searched?'

'No,' I said. 'I don't think that.'

'Then where is it?' Penny folded her arms and gave me her best hard glare. 'If there isn't any thief, what reason could anyone have to hide the mummy?'

'To confuse the issue and mess with our heads,' I said. 'So we'd waste time arguing about the mystery of the missing mummy, instead of concentrating on what really matters. Which is who killed George Cardavan.'

Penny thought about that, then unfolded her arms and nodded reluctantly. 'Yes. That makes sense. You're right. Do not smile, or I will beat you severely about the head and shoulders.'

'We'll find the mummy, eventually,' I said. 'Either the killer will tell us when we catch him, or just knowing who it is will tell us where to look.'

'It must be wonderful to be so optimistic all the time,' said Penny.

I considered the point. 'Yes, it is.'

We grinned at each other, and then looked round the empty room.

'Why,' I said, 'do people always insist on going off on their own? When it should be obvious to everyone that they'd be safer as part of a group.'

'It's human nature,' said Penny. 'Look out for yourself, and to hell with everyone else.'

'It's a wonder to me you've survived this long as a species,' I said. 'Did you happen to notice . . . Stuart seemed more upset over George's death than any member of the family?'

'Hardly surprising, when you look at the family,' said Penny. 'They've all spent too long concentrating on the collection, instead of each other. Take Marjorie. From tears and hysterics to icy calm in no time at all. Even for a gold-digging trophy wife, that's a staggeringly self-centred reaction. And Chloe seems more interested in interrogating you than on what's going on around her. Even after her father's death.'

She stopped abruptly, as a thought struck her.

145

'Do you suppose Stuart had some reason to believe George was in danger? And that's why he wanted you here?'

'I don't think so,' I said. 'He's always been more concerned about protecting his wife.'

Penny pulled a face. 'It feels strange calling him Stuart, instead of Colonel.'

'Stranger than you know,' I said. 'The Colonel's job is to pass on orders and information to the agents he runs. To send us out on assignments that might well get us killed. He isn't supposed to get close to any of us, for his protection as well as ours. He certainly isn't supposed to ask his agents for personal favours.'

'So why did Stuart come to you for help?' said Penny.

'I'm still working on that,' I said.

'Could this be some kind of trap, or test? A chance to watch you operate at close quarters so he can figure out what you are?'

'If that was the idea, things have got considerably out of hand.'

'Maybe . . . he just didn't have anyone else he felt he could turn to,' said Penny.

'It can be that kind of life sometimes in this business,' I said. 'Sometimes it's not who you know but who you can trust. We all walk alone . . . Except for me, of course. Because I have you.'

'Nice save, sweetie,' said Penny. 'Now, what about Professor Rose? Could he have been abducted?'

'If there's no thief in the house, who could have taken him?'

'There's always the mummy . . .'

'No there isn't,' I said firmly. 'Much more likely Rose believed he knew where the mummy was and wanted to find it himself.'

Penny frowned. 'Then why not take Stuart with him for protection?'

'I don't think Rose trusts anyone else where the collection is concerned.'

'Could Stuart have done something to Rose?'

'He could, but I can't see why he'd want to.'

'The Colonel is running some kind of game,' Penny said wisely. 'He brought you here for a reason, and I don't think we know what it is yet.'

'He doesn't seem to be watching me more than anyone else,' I said. 'Though I have been very careful not to give him anything unusual to watch.'

'But what if you had to do something out of the ordinary? I mean, in order to save someone's life?'

'Then I'll do what I have to, and worry about it afterwards.'

'Does the Organization know what you are?' said Penny.

'They've never given me any reason to believe that,' I said. 'But since I have no idea who or what they really are, who knows what they know? I don't think they care, as long as I remain useful to them.'

'If push came to shove,' Penny said determinedly, 'Who do you think they'd back? You or the Colonel?'

'The difference between me and the Colonel,' I said, 'Is that they know where to find him. I can walk out any time and disappear back into the world . . . and they know it.' I looked at her seriously. 'Penny, if it all did go bad and I had to go on the run again . . . I couldn't take you with me.'

She met my gaze steadily. 'Why not? Because I'd slow you down?'

'No, because you would have to give up everything and everyone you know. Walk away from your whole life forever. I couldn't do that to you.'

'But I wouldn't have a life without you,' said Penny.

We looked at each other for a long time. Sometimes you don't need to say anything.

And then I turned sharply to look at the closed door. I could hear the sound of running feet out in the corridor, heading our way. Lots of people running. Penny's head came up as she started to hear them, too. I looked at the chair by the door and realized I'd never got round to jamming it back in place. The door slammed open and Marjorie burst in, travelling so fast I had to jump back out of her way so she wouldn't crash into me. She stumbled to a halt, breathing harshly, her eyes wide with panic. She collapsed into the nearest chair and tried to say something to me, but couldn't get the words out.

Bernard and Susan were next through the door, moving remarkably quickly for people their age. Bernard's face was flushed from exertion, but his hands were clenched into fists; ready to defend himself and Susan. She was moaning to herself, in between gasps for breath, her face slack with shock. They helped each other across the room to their favourite chairs, and dropped into them.

148

Chloe and Stuart were the last to arrive. Moving at a more than reasonable pace, but not actually running. She looked shaken, he looked even more protective than usual. Stuart saw Chloe to the nearest chair, then hurried back to the door, slammed it shut and jammed the waiting chair into place. Giving it a good hard shove, to make sure nothing would move it.

'What is it?' said Penny. 'What's happened? Is someone after you?'

'Where are Nicholas and Caroline?' I said.

Penny looked round sharply, as she realized they were missing. I looked from one traumatized face to another. Their breathing was slowing now as they regained their composure, but none of them said anything. They exchanged glances, as though they all wanted someone else to speak first. And I thought I sensed something that might have been guilt. What had they done? What had they run away from? I looked at Stuart, and he faced me squarely.

'It started with footsteps on the landing outside our rooms,' he said. 'Human footsteps, but . . . there was something wrong with them.'

'They sounded soft,' said Chloe. 'Strangely muffled . . . It was horrible.'

'Like the cloth-wrapped feet of a mummy?' said Penny.

I was ready to say something sharp to her, but didn't when I saw how the others were looking at each other. None of them was ready to say it out loud, but they were all thinking the same as Penny. I drew up a chair facing them, and gestured for Penny and Stuart to sit down too.

'All right,' I said. 'Talk me through it.'

'The footsteps started outside our room,' said Chloe. 'They just seemed to be there suddenly, with no warning. Someone tried the handle of our door, but Stuart had a chair in place. I called out, asking who it was, but no one answered. I went over to the door to listen, and heard the footsteps move on down the corridor.'

'They tried my door,' said Marjorie. 'But I had a chair jammed up against it, too. Whoever it was rattled the door hard, trying to force it open, but the chair held. I couldn't say anything. I was too scared.'

'Then they came to our room,' said Susan. Her eyes were red and puffy from where she'd been crying again. Her voice was a very small thing, almost wiped out by shock and strain. 'Bernard had put a chair against the door first thing, thank God. They kept trying the door handle, turning it back and forth and pushing against the door, but it wouldn't budge. I shouted for them to go away. They didn't say anything.'

'I was ready to go out and confront them,' said Bernard. 'But Susan wouldn't let me.'

'By then I had my ear pressed against our door, listening to what was going on,' said Stuart. 'I was ready to go out too . . .'

'But I wouldn't let him,' said Chloe. 'I'd back Stuart against any man . . . but this didn't sound like any man.'

'Eventually, whoever or whatever it was realized they couldn't get into any of our rooms,' said Stuart. 'The muffled footsteps moved away, back down the corridor towards the stairs, until I

150

couldn't hear them any more. I pulled the chair away from our door, opened it, and looked out. There was no sign of anyone, no sign anyone had ever been there. I called out to the others and told them it was safe to come out. And they did.'

'I didn't want to,' said Marjorie. 'I was so scared I was trembling like a leaf, but I was more afraid of being on my own. You don't know what it was like, listening to those awful sounds! Knowing something monstrous wanted to get in, to get to me.'

'We gathered together on the landing,' said Chloe. 'We were all really shaken. I thought I was brave, until then. I mean, I've seen some things but . . .'

'None of you saw what made the noises?' I said.

'No,' said Stuart. 'No one opened their door at any point. I'm sure. I would have heard.'

I thought about that. Could any of them have opened their door and gone up and down the corridor trying doors, and then sneaked back into their room, without being heard? It didn't seem likely. And what could have been so wrong about those footsteps to affect everyone so badly?

'That was when I realized Nicholas and Caroline hadn't come out of their room,' said Stuart. 'I banged on their door. Shouted their names, told them it was safe to come out. They didn't answer. I was ready to kick their door in, but . . .'

'Marjorie had hysterics,' said Chloe. 'Saying over and over that she had to get back to the drawing room, where she'd felt safe. And once she started, that was all any of us could think of.'

'I was upset!' said Marjorie.

151

'I led the way down,' said Stuart. 'I couldn't let them run through the house on their own. But I didn't go fast enough for all of them.'

'I was scared!' said Marjorie. 'I wasn't thinking . . .'

'So I took up the rear, to watch everyone's back,' said Stuart. 'Keeping Chloe close to me, for safety. Just in case . . . something bad was loose in the house.'

'You left Nicholas and Caroline behind?' I said. 'No wonder you all looked so guilty.'

'I had to protect the people with me!' said Stuart. 'Now they're safe, I'll go back up again. Check on Nicholas and Caroline, make sure they're all right.'

'Anything could have happened to them,' said Penny.

'I didn't want to leave them!' said Chloe. 'He's my brother! We just got . . . swept up in the moment.'

'You don't know what it was like up there,' said Marjorie. 'It was horrible . . .'

'Stuart,' I said, 'You stand guard over these people. Penny and I will check out the top floor.'

'I'm going with you,' said Stuart.

'No!' Chloe said immediately. 'You can't leave us!'

'Someone's got to be in charge here,' I said to Stuart. 'If only to keep them from doing something stupid.'

'You're not armed,' said Stuart. 'You should take something with you.'

'Whoever or whatever you heard, it couldn't get past a closed door,' I said. 'So it can't be that

152

strong. You're sure you only heard one set of footsteps?'

I looked round. Everyone nodded.

'They sounded . . . weirdly light,' said Stuart. 'As though there was no real weight to them. Like a ghost walking.'

'Or a dead thing,' said Marjorie.

Everyone was nodding now.

'Once we're gone,' I said to Stuart, 'wedge the chair under the door again and keep everyone in here. No one is to leave this room, and don't open the door to anyone but me. I'll yell out, so you can be sure it's me.'

'Why don't we all just leave?' Marjorie said loudly. 'Just . . . get in our cars and go. This house is a death trap.'

I looked at Stuart. 'Is that what you think we should do?'

He looked at Chloe. She shook her head stubbornly. Her face was still unhealthily pale, but she was back in command of herself. 'I need to know what's happened to Nicky and his wife. We're safe in here, and Security is on the way.'

I didn't look at Stuart. We both knew no one was coming.

'No one leaves this house,' Chloe said flatly. 'Not until we find out who killed my father.'

'You still think it was one of us!' Marjorie said angrily. 'How could any of us do something like that? It was inhuman. We have to go!'

'Once you've left the house,' I said, 'you could go anywhere.'

'He's right,' said Bernard. 'We stay. All of us.'

Marjorie looked like she still wanted to argue,

but no one was on her side. She sank back in her chair and scowled sullenly.

'As soon as Penny and I have determined what's happened, we'll come back down and tell you,' I said. 'Then we can decide what to do next.'

I got to my feet, and so did Penny and Stuart. I looked round the room. No one wanted to look at me. I pulled the chair away, opened the door, and looked out. The long corridor stretched away, disappearing into its shadows, silent and empty. I stepped out into the corridor, and Penny was quickly there at my side. Almost trembling with eagerness to go chasing into danger, so she could stare it in the face and ask it pointed questions. Sometimes I wonder which of us is supposed to be looking after who. The door slammed shut behind us, and I heard the chair being jammed back into place. Someone wasn't taking any chances.

'Is it just me,' said Penny, 'or does this corridor feel more than usually quiet?'

'Silent as the grave,' I said.

'Not really helping!' She looked at me. 'Can you hear anything? Smell anything . . . unusual?'

'No,' I said. 'Let's go upstairs and see if that changes.'

'Fine!' said Penny. 'I'll punch them in the head, and then you kick them when they're down.'

'Sounds like a plan to me,' I said.

We strode off down the corridor, heading for the first set of stairs. By now I knew where every room in the house was, and the quickest way to get there. Our footsteps sounded clearly on the wooden floorboards, nothing soft or muffled about them. The shadows were still deep and dark, but I was getting used to that. And as long as I didn't look at the artefacts and exhibits, they couldn't look back at me.

'Do you think Nicholas and Caroline are dead?' Penny said quietly. 'There could be any number of reasons why they didn't answer.'

'Any number,' I said. 'But not many good ones.'

We moved quickly through the silent house, keeping a watchful eye on our surroundings, but there wasn't any sight or sound of anyone else. We hurried up one set of stairs after another, and by the time we hit the third flight Penny was seriously out of breath and puffing like a steam train with asthma. She waved for me to go on, but I wouldn't leave her on her own. I waited patiently as she slumped against the banister, getting her breath back. Finally Penny nodded stiffly, and we set off again.

'Why can't people be killed in bungalows?' she growled. 'Everywhere we go, it's always stairways and corridors . . . And in future, you might want to consider going armed.'

'I have done in the past,' I said. 'When the mission demanded it. But when you carry a weapon, that's always going to be your first response to a tense situation.'

'Right now, that doesn't seem like such a bad thing,' said Penny.

'But what if I were to glimpse something moving, out of the corner of my eye,' I said, 'and then opened fire to protect myself or you? Only to find the moving thing was Professor Rose. He's still around here, somewhere.'

'That is kind of odd, isn't it?' said Penny. 'I mean, shouldn't we have bumped into him by now? Why hasn't he made himself known? Where could he be that he hasn't heard all the commotion and come to ask what's going on?' She looked at me sharply. 'Do you think he's dead, too?'

'No point in guessing,' I said. 'In a tense situation, it's always too easy to jump straight to the worst-case scenario.'

'To be fair,' said Penny, 'that is how most of our cases turn out.'

'Then let's try to be optimistic,' I said.

We stopped at the top of the stairs and looked down the third floor landing. It all seemed quiet and empty. I did spot one thing: the floor here was carpeted, as opposed to the wooden floorboards in the rest of the house. Which might have contributed to the muffled sound of the footsteps. Penny leaned in close to murmur in my ear.

'Can you smell blood?'

'It's been hard for me to smell anything in this house,' I said. 'But up here, away from the collection, the scents are fainter and more diffused. I can smell flowers in vases, soaps and perfumes . . . but no blood.'

'You can smell all that, through closed doors?'

'Yes.'

'Decidedly weird. No blood . . . That's a good thing, isn't it?'

'Usually,' I said.

Nicholas and Caroline's door was still closed. I knocked loudly and called out to them, but there was no reply. I tried the handle, and it turned easily. I eased the door open. There was no chair in place to stop me.

'Do you think it was open all along?' said Penny.

'Could have been,' I said. 'Stuart said he was ready to kick it in but never got a chance. Why isn't there a chair jammed against it? Nicholas and Caroline had just as many reasons to be cautious as everyone else . . . I'm going in. You stay by the door.'

I pushed the door all the way open and stepped carefully into the room. Nicholas and Caroline were lying on the floor, side by side, not moving. Penny made a noise behind me, but stayed where she was. I looked slowly round the room. No sign of a struggle, nothing out of place. Nicholas and Caroline hadn't even got round to picking up the clothes they'd left scattered around the room when they changed for dinner. Perhaps they never got the chance. I knelt down beside each body in turn and checked for vital signs, but they only confirmed what I already knew.

'They're dead, aren't they?' said Penny.

'Yes,' I said. 'But not a mark on either of them. No obvious cause of death. Their faces look surprisingly peaceful.'

'Caroline had a poker to protect herself,' said Penny.

I looked around. The poker was lying on the bed, as though it had been dropped there quite casually. Nothing about it to suggest it had ever been raised in anger.

'Can I come in?' said Penny.

'All right,' I said. 'But be careful. This is a crime scene, let's not contaminate things more than we have to.'

Penny entered the room one careful step at a time. She looked at the bodies and shook her head sadly. 'This is . . . eerie. They could almost be sleeping. It's like they just collapsed and died, for no reason.'

'There's always a reason,' I said.

'Could they have been frightened to death by the mummy?'

'What we saw in the sarcophagus wasn't exactly scary,' I said.

'It's probably different when you open your bedroom door to find it standing there grinning at you,' said Penny.

'Possibly,' I said. 'But Caroline had her poker. And she wasn't the kind to scare easily. She would have gone down fighting.'

'Whoever Stuart and the others heard, wasn't strong enough to force open their doors,' said Penny. 'So Nicholas and Caroline must have opened the door to their killer. Why would they do that?'

'Only one answer makes sense,' I said. 'They knew who it was. And didn't see that person as any kind of threat.'

'Then the killer must have identified himself, or herself, through the closed door,' said Penny. 'Why only speak to Nicholas and Caroline? And why kill them, rather than the others?'

'Because they opened the door,' I said. 'Question is did this happen before the killer continued on down the corridor to try the other doors, or did it happen afterwards? If the killer spoke to them first, why didn't the others hear? They heard the footsteps clearly enough.'

'You mean Nicholas and Caroline could have already been dead when Stuart was knocking on their door?' said Penny. 'If that's the case, he couldn't have saved them anyway.'

'He didn't know that when he abandoned them,' I said.

'This case just gets more and more complicated,' said Penny.

'Yes,' I said. 'It does. What happened in this room is completely different to what happened to George. He was bludgeoned to death. Nicholas and Caroline look like they died in their sleep.'

'On the floor?'

'More likely in mid-step.'

'Remember the stories from Egypt?' said Penny. 'The local people who died because of the curse from no obvious cause!'

'I hadn't forgotten,' I said. 'The way George died suggested rage, even a desire to punish. What happened here feels more . . . calculated. And while I can see all kinds of reasons why people might want George dead, why Nicholas and Caroline? They had no money; they'd even been cut out of the will, according to Marjorie. And I don't see how they could have made an enemy out of anyone here, when they hadn't been back to visit the family in ages.'

'Perhaps they saw something concerning the first murder,' said Penny. 'Something they didn't realize was significant. But still important enough that the killer had to silence them before they could blurt it out and give the game away.'

'Possibly,' I said. 'But why such a different manner of death?'

'Because the killer wasn't mad at them?' said Penny. 'Killing George was personal, but silencing two witnesses was just business.'

'George was beaten to death,' I said. 'I can understand that. But I have no idea how Nicholas and Caroline died. It's as though their hearts just failed or they simply stopped breathing.'

'Could it be natural causes?' Penny said tentatively.

'Together? Simultaneously and in exactly the same way? I don't think so.'

'Poison, then?' said Penny. 'Some kind of gas sprayed into their faces? I saw that in a spy movie once.'

'A poison would leave some sign,' I said. 'In the face, eyes or lips . . . And I'm not smelling anything unusual.'

'Injections?'

I looked at her. 'Can you really see them standing still for an injection? Bare your arm, please, it's time for your mummy immunization shots . . .'

'Well, if you're going to put it like that . . .' And then she stopped abruptly, and her eyes widened. 'Oh, Ishmael . . . Could this be another vampire? Could something have just sucked the life out of them?'

I knelt down and examined both necks carefully. 'No bite marks. I suppose there could be more than one kind of vampire . . .' I got to my feet again. 'Let's not get ahead of ourselves. We need to go back and tell the others what's happened.'

'And leave Nicholas and Caroline here?'

'You want to carry them downstairs?'

'I don't want to leave them here on their own!'

'They're not here,' I said. 'All that's here is what they left behind.'

We went back down the three flights of stairs. Not hurrying, because the sense of urgency was gone. Going back down into the heavy scents generated by the collection was like descending into a fog, filling my head with ancient smells. We strode through the gloomy corridors side by side, and didn't see or hear anything along the way. Finally, I banged on the drawing room door and said my name loudly. There was a long pause, so Penny spoke up too. I heard the chair being dragged away, and then the door opened just a crack so Stuart could look out. He pulled the door back just enough to admit us, and the moment we were inside he slammed it shut and jammed the chair back in place. He even kicked it a few times, to make sure it was wedged in properly. I raised an eyebrow.

'Did something happen while we were gone? Did you hear the footsteps again?'

'No,' said Stuart. 'Just being cautious.'

I broke the news about Nicholas and Caroline. Susan immediately collapsed in floods of tears. Bernard had to comfort her. He always seemed more together when he was thinking of someone else. He patted Susan's arm awkwardly, but she

161

didn't even look at him. Interestingly, Bernard looked more angry than scared or upset.

'Nicholas wasn't a bad sort, really,' he said gruffly. 'I had more time for him than his father. George never could see that the lad just needed some space, to be his own man and go his own way. When I get my hands on the bastard that did this . . .'

Chloe sat slumped in her chair, as though all the strength had gone out of her. She stared straight ahead, too crushed even to cry.

'Nicky. Oh, Nicky, I'm so sorry . . .'

'It's not your fault,' said Stuart.

'Yes it is,' said Chloe. 'I'm the one who persuaded him to come back. He didn't want to. He was always terrified of this house. But I told him I didn't trust Marjorie, that she was using her influence on father to steal our inheritance. If I hadn't insisted he come home so we could work on father together, he'd still be alive.'

'You never liked me,' said Marjorie. There was a certain satisfaction in her voice at having her suspicions confirmed.

'You stole our father from us!' said Chloe.

She surged up out of her chair and threw herself at Marjorie. She grabbed a good handful of Marjorie's hair, and drew back her other hand to make a fist. Marjorie shrieked pitifully. Stuart grabbed hold of Chloe and pulled her away. She turned on Stuart, and then collapsed against him, burying her face in his shoulder.

'You saw her!' Marjorie said triumphantly, rearranging her hair with unsteady hands. 'The bitch tried to kill me!'

'Shut up, Marjorie,' said Stuart.

Chloe pushed herself away from Stuart. She still wasn't crying, and when she spoke her voice was distant but steady.

'Nicky was always so scared of this place. He had a dream once that told him he'd die here. I should have listened to him.'

Stuart quietly persuaded her to sit down again, and then came over to me.

'We have to leave the house. All of us. It's not safe here. Someone is killing people and we have no defence against them.'

'This is no time to panic, boy!' Bernard said sternly. 'We only have to hang on till Security get here. Can't be long now.'

'They're not coming,' said Stuart. 'I told them not to.'

The whole room went quiet. They all looked at him incredulously.

'Why the hell did you do that?' said Bernard.

'I was afraid they'd complicate things,' said Stuart. 'There are security issues here . . . I know none of you want to hear that, but it doesn't alter the facts.'

'I think we can assume security issues aren't as important now,' I said carefully.

'Of course not,' said Stuart.

'Then we're leaving,' Bernard said forcefully. 'Right now, no arguments. Come along, Susan.'

Everyone stood up. Stuart looked at me.

'I had to protect my family . . . but now it's time to go. Lead the way, Ishmael. There's cars enough for all of us.'

Stuart was right, people's safety had to come

163

first. I pulled the chair away, opened the door, and peered out into the corridor.

'All clear, no one around. We head straight for the front door. No stopping, no side trips.'

'I don't know,' Susan said unhappily. Bernard had got her on her feet, but she was still dithering, refusing to move. 'What if that awful mummy is still out there? Waiting for us?'

'We're a big group,' I said. 'We can handle one mummy.'

'What if that's the last thing Nicholas and Caroline ever thought . . .?' said Chloe.

'We don't know the mummy had anything to do with their deaths,' I said.

'We don't know that it didn't!' said Marjorie. 'I never liked having that thing in the house. Everything was fine until George brought it here.'

'Are you saying you believe in the curse?' said Stuart.

'Don't you?' said Marjorie. 'Something wants all of us dead!'

No one had anything to say to that.

'Professor Rose is still wandering around on his own somewhere,' I said. 'Are we leaving him behind?'

'We'll call out to him as we go,' said Stuart. 'If he hasn't the common sense to come and join us, that's his problem.' And then he stopped and looked at me. 'Or are you suggesting Rose might be the killer?'

'Let's just say, I'd feel a lot happier if I knew where he was,' I said.

I stepped out of the door, gestured for the others to stay put for a moment, and called out

164

to Professor Rose. My voice seemed to echo on and on in the hush, but there was no response. I gestured for the others to come out and join me. Penny was immediately there at my side. Marjorie was next out of the room, all set mouth and nervous impatience. Bernard got Susan moving with gruff encouraging words. Stuart and Chloe brought up the rear.

For a long moment nobody moved. They all just stood there and looked at me. I gave them my best reassuring smile, and started off.

I led the way through the dimly lit corridors, following the map in my memory, heading for the entrance hall by the shortest possible route. Stuart chivvied everyone on from the rear to make sure they kept up. Standard military thinking: keep people occupied so they don't have time to feel scared. I kept a careful watch, but there was no one around. Just the endless painted eyes of artefacts watching from the sides.

We reached the entrance hall without incident. The quick pace had taken a lot out of the group, but fortunately that meant they didn't have enough breath left to complain. Penny's suitcases and mine were still standing in the middle of the hall where we'd left them. It felt as if we'd left them there days ago. I strode quickly past them to open the front door. It was locked. I gave the door a good rattling, but it wouldn't budge. The others milled around speechlessly, horrified by such a betrayal when escape seemed so close. Penny and Stuart came forward to join me.

'How can it be locked?' said Penny.

'Someone doesn't want us to leave,' I said. 'George's house keys are still missing. Presumably taken from his body.'

'Why would a mummy do that?' said Penny.

'It wouldn't,' I said.

'None of us could have locked this door,' said Stuart. 'We've all been together.'

'Not all of the time,' I said. 'We don't know when the door was locked, and we can't trust everyone to tell the truth where their partners are concerned.'

'You think I'd lie about something like this?' said Stuart.

'Of course,' I said. 'Didn't you bring us here in the first place to protect Chloe at all costs?'

'Wouldn't you lie to protect Penny?' said Stuart.

'I've never needed to,' I said.

'That's not an answer.'

'I know.'

I turned back to consider the locked door. It was really large and really heavy.

Penny moved in close beside me. 'Could you break it down,' she murmured, 'if you have to?'

'Maybe,' I said quietly. 'But not without drawing a lot of attention.' I looked back at Stuart. 'How many other exits to the house are there?'

'Just one,' he said. 'The back door, on the other side of the house. Follow me, I know the way.'

He took the lead and hurried us along. No one objected. The others were genuinely scared now. Being locked inside a house is almost as scary as being locked out. Especially when you don't know who's got the keys. I brought up the rear,

166

glaring at every shadow. When we finally got to the back door, it was locked too. Another large and very heavy door. I looked it over carefully, while Stuart did his best to calm and reassure the others. Penny looked to me for answers.

'Someone was thinking ahead,' I said. 'They didn't want anyone leaving.'

'But why?' said Penny.

'I think we can now safely assume it's not about stealing an expensive mummy,' I said. 'A thief would want us gone, to make it easier to escape with the prize. Someone wants us all dead . . . And I have no idea why.'

'There is the curse . . .' said Penny.

'No there isn't!' I said. 'And even if there was, what would it want with you and me?'

'You've been thinking about it!' said Penny.

'Much against my will,' I said.

Stuart came over to join us. 'We have to do something. The family's getting restive. I don't know how much longer I can keep them from doing something stupid.'

'Could we smash a window?' I said. 'Get out that way?'

'All the windows are security-sealed,' said Chloe. She came forward to stand with Stuart, doing her best to hold on to her composure. 'Unbreakable glass, to protect the collection.'

'Including the living quarters on the top floor?' I said.

'All of them,' said Chloe. 'Once the value of the collection reached a certain point, grandfather became a little . . . paranoid. About thieves and other collectors. He had all the old windows taken

167

out and replaced, while we were away. The first we knew about it was when we got back and grandfather presented us with a *fait accompli.*'

'He didn't discuss it with the family, because he knew they wouldn't agree,' said Stuart. 'Bernard always went his own way. That was part of the problem.'

'The safety of the collection had to come first,' said Chloe. 'Father always said he was going to put in some safety features, but once the collection was his he kept coming up with excuses to put it off. This damned collection . . . It does something to otherwise sane and sensible people. It clouds their judgement.'

I turned away from the locked back door. I didn't want to try breaking it open until I absolutely had to. Preferably without witnesses. But it didn't feel safe to keep everyone just standing around.

'Call the security people,' I said to Stuart. 'Tell them they're needed. Now.'

He nodded and took out his mobile phone. And then we all had to watch him walk up and down the corridor, trying for a signal. He finally got through, talked quietly and urgently, and then put the phone away.

'They're coming,' he said flatly. 'I told them to bring equipment to break into the house if need be. But it'll take them at least an hour to get here.'

'You should have called them immediately after George was killed!' said Bernard. 'They'd have been here by now.'

'I suggest we go back to the drawing room,'

I said. 'We can sit tight there till help arrives. The security people will get you away safely, and then Stuart and Penny and I will tear this place apart till we get to the bottom of what's happening. Unless you know a better place to hole up, Stuart?'

'No, the drawing room has to be the best bet,' said Stuart. 'It's on the ground floor, easily defendable, with just the one door and no windows. We can hold out there for an hour or so.'

'What do you mean by "or so"?' said Marjorie.

'In theory, the security people should be here inside an hour,' said Stuart. 'But they've never had to do it before. I kept telling George he should schedule some training drills . . .'

'What about Professor Rose?' Penny said suddenly. 'Are we just going to leave him wandering around the house on his own?'

'If he comes to the drawing room and identifies himself properly, we'll let him in,' said Stuart. 'But I'm not sending out a search party. From now on, we stick together and watch each other's backs.'

Penny looked at me, expecting me to volunteer to go off and find Rose. But I didn't.

'You do think he's dead!' she said accusingly.

'Either that or bait in a trap,' I said.

'For who?' said Penny.

'Good question,' I said.

'Since when have you been afraid to take a risk, Ishmael Jones?' said Penny.

'Someone is playing a game in this house,' I said steadily. 'And I'm not playing until I've got a better idea of the rules.'

Six
Hidden in Plain Sight

We turned on all the lights in the drawing room, made sure the chair was jammed up tight against the door, and then sat stiffly in our chairs and waited. Either for Security to turn up and rescue us or for something to happen. No one seemed to feel like talking. We all kept an eye on the door, straining our ears for any sound out in the corridor. The slow ticking of the old-fashioned clock on the mantelpiece dominated the room, counting down the minutes till our rescuers could get to us. I would much rather have been out in the house doing something, but I couldn't just go off and leave the others. So I sat as still as I could and listened to people breathing, an occasional stirring in a chair or a suddenly crossed leg, and now and again the clink of bottle on glass.

I was probably the only one in that room who wasn't particularly worried. I'd seen my share of dead bodies and faced far more dangerous things than an elusive thief or a perambulating mummy. All I wanted now was to keep as many people as I could alive until help arrived. I kept a surreptitious eye on everyone, trying to get a sense of how they were coping. It still seemed likely to me that someone in the room was the killer; and yet everywhere I looked they all seemed far more like victims the killer hadn't got round to yet. Fear and tension filled the room, along with barely concealed distrust. No one was looking at anyone directly, but they were all sneaking glances at each other when they thought no one was looking.

Bernard was drinking heavily again. He had his own bottle of whisky and a glass, and was knocking it back steadily with no real appearance of pleasure. As though it was just medicine. Now Susan no longer needed his support and protection, his ability to concentrate was slipping away again and was limited to just what was in front of him. His gaze moved uncertainly round the room, as though he was surprised to find himself surrounded by people he wasn't sure he recognized. I kept a careful watch on him. He was still a large man, large enough to make him dangerous if he ever really lost control.

Soon enough, Bernard slammed his glass down hard on the arm of his chair, breaking the silence with a voice that was as much confused as angry.

'Where's George?' he said loudly. 'This is his house now. He should be here looking after his guests, not leaving it up to me!'

There was an awkward pause, and then Susan leaned forward to smile steadily at her husband. Her voice was entirely calm, as though nothing was wrong.

'George is with Professor Rose, dear, discussing the latest additions to the collection. You remember the professor.'

It wasn't clear that Bernard did, but he nodded

171

grumpily, filled his glass again, and went back to his drinking. Glowering at no one in particular. Chloe couldn't look at him. Stuart looked like he wanted to say something, but didn't know what to say. Susan levered herself painfully up out of her chair, wandered round the room for a while, and finally ended up by the door. Penny and I looked at each other, and then got up and went over to join her.

'When he gets like this, it's easier to tell him a simple lie,' Susan said quietly. 'It saves time and avoids arguments. He hates being confronted with how forgetful he's getting.'

'How long has he been like this?' said Penny.

'Oh, he's been drifting away from me for over a year now,' said Susan. She seemed to be addressing the closed door as much as Penny or me. Perhaps that made it easier. 'He gets more . . . troubled every day. There's less and less of him all the time. When we went up to change for dinner earlier, I had to leave him for a moment, just to go to the bathroom, and when I got back he was sitting on the edge of the bed in his underwear, almost in tears. Because he couldn't remember which clothes he was supposed to be putting on. I had to dress him. Just as I do every morning.'

She shook her head slowly, bitterly. 'I never thought our life would come to this. That I'd have to do . . . this sort of thing for him. That's not my husband, I find myself thinking . . . Not the man I knew and loved. But some of him emerges now and again, just often enough to make it really cruel.'

She didn't wait for me or Penny to say anything. She'd had her moment of weakness, and now she picked up her burden of duty again and went back to sit beside what was left of her husband. Who didn't appear to notice she'd ever left his side.

Penny and I had just sat down again when Marjorie stirred in her chair. She'd settled herself some distance from the rest of us, with a bottle of gin all to herself. Like Bernard she was getting through glass after glass, as though it was just something to do. Slumped ungainly in her chair, Marjorie was a sloppy drinker, spilling the stuff down her front and smearing her make-up, and not giving a damn. She suddenly started speaking, without prompting. Perhaps the silence bothered her, or perhaps she just thought it was her turn to say something. Her words didn't seem to be aimed at anyone in particular.

'I never liked this house. Draughty old dump, no proper amenities, miles from anywhere civilized, anywhere fun . . . I never wanted to live here, but George said we had to because his father had lost his mind. Because someone had to look after the collection. My George, my lovely George . . . I wanted him, so I had to take everything that came with him. The house, the family, the collection . . . We could have been so happy together . . . but there was all this shit that came with him.'

She raised her head suddenly, to glare around the room with eyes that weren't crying only because there was so much anger in them. 'He'd still be alive if it wasn't for you! And the house, and the stupid bloody collection!'

No one said anything, so she went back to her drinking.

'People can always surprise you,' Penny said quietly.

'Rarely in a good way,' I said.

'She honestly did care for father,' said Chloe. 'But who knew?'

'She fitted the cliché so perfectly we never thought to look beyond it,' said Stuart.

Chloe leaned forward in her chair. 'Marjorie . . . Marjorie!'

'What?' Marjorie's head jerked up, and it took her a moment to focus on Chloe. 'What do you want? I'm busy.'

'Why did you cut everyone else out of the will if you didn't care about the collection?'

Marjorie snorted loudly. 'I didn't! That was all George's doing . . . He was fed up with the lot of you. Said none of you were worthy of the collection. He just wanted me to make sure the collection would go to someone who'd look after it properly.' She snorted again, but her heart wasn't in it. 'I tried to tell him I didn't give a damn about any of that. I only cared for him . . . my lovely George.'

She went back to brooding over her gin, and Chloe sank back in her chair. From the look on her face, she had a lot to think about. I turned to Stuart.

'You keep staring at the door. Is there a problem?'

'I'm not convinced a single chair is enough to keep out a determined enemy,' he said, in a voice that was pure Colonel. 'Perhaps we should drag

174

some of the heavier furniture over and put together a proper barricade.'

'I've seen that done before, on other missions,' I said. 'By people who thought it would protect them. And yet somehow it never seems to help much. Besides, it's always possible that at some point we might need to leave in a hurry.'

Stuart looked at me sharply. 'What do you mean? Are you thinking someone might find another way into this room and attack us?'

'Possibly,' I said. 'But rather more likely . . . What if one of us is the killer? And what if that person has decided that when help arrives they can't afford to have the rest of us around to contradict whatever story the killer has in mind to explain everything? A single survivor would face much more sympathy.'

'You have to admire the way his mind works,' said Penny. 'No one can be as scary as Ishmael when he's being logical.'

'We might need to get that door open in a hurry . . .' I said to Stuart.

But he was already looking at the door and nodding in agreement. This kind of forethought appealed to his military training.

Chloe turned suddenly to look at me. 'Given that we may not survive this evening, are you ready to tell me who you really are, Ishmael?'

'Chloe, dear,' said Stuart, 'I promised Ishmael anonymity when he agreed to help us.'

'I know, dear,' said Chloe. 'And that really was very sweet of you, but this isn't a time for secrets. We could start with you, if you like. You've been telling us for years that you left Black Heir to

175

take up a job in the Government, but did you really think I was ever going to believe that? You're not the civil-servant type. You walked out on your beloved Army because they wanted to stick you behind a desk. Don't forget I work for Black Heir! I know when someone's hiding something. I used my contacts . . . and while none of them could find out exactly who you work for, just the levels of security involved narrowed it down to a few very obvious, very secret organizations. I'm not an idiot, you know.'

'I never thought you were,' said Stuart. 'I would have told you, if I could. But it wouldn't have been safe. For you, or for me. Some things are secret for a reason.'

'I know,' said Chloe. 'That's why I stopped digging.'

She turned back to me. 'I'm damned if I'm going to die with my curiosity unsatisfied. Do you work for my husband, and whoever he works for?'

'We're in the same line of business,' I said carefully. 'And it really wouldn't be safe for you to know any more than that.'

'Even now?' said Chloe.

'Perhaps especially now,' I said. 'There's nothing like shared danger to bring people together and make them feel like opening up to each other. To talk about the things they always wanted to talk about, although they know they really shouldn't. But I am determined that all of us are going to survive. So we shouldn't bring up anything we might have cause to regret later.'

Chloe looked at Penny. 'Is he always this . . . professional?'

'When it comes to secrets,' Penny said solemnly, 'Ishmael is in a class of his own.'

'I wouldn't argue with that!' said Stuart.

'Why are you so keen to know everything about me, Chloe?' I said.

She smiled sourly. 'Because I never get to go out in the field. I just move the paperwork around, making sure everyone is where they're supposed to be. I've seen some of the stuff our people bring in . . . but never know where it comes from. It was obvious you specialize in field work, and I wanted you to tell me if it's as exciting as I always believed. But now I've had a taste of the real thing, I just want it all to be over . . .'

She looked at me steadily. 'You saw Nicky and Caroline. Are you sure they didn't suffer?'

'No,' said Penny, 'they just died. There wasn't a mark on them. Like the Egyptians in Professor Rose's story.'

'Where is that man?' said Stuart. 'We should have heard from him by now. It's not that big a house.'

'Is he dead, do you think?' said Chloe, still looking at me.

'First rule in this business,' I said. 'Never assume anyone's dead until you've seen the body. And even then it's usually a good idea to give it a good hard poke with a stick, just to be on the safe side. But given how long it's been since anyone saw Professor Rose, I would have to say the odds are not good . . .'

'Four people dead, in such a short time,' said Chloe. 'Father, Nicky, Caroline and Professor Rose. I wish the security people would get here.'

She didn't look at Stuart, but I could tell from his face that he thought she blamed him for not calling them in sooner. He cleared his throat, in that clear and emphatic way they must teach in officer school as a prelude to changing the subject.

'I really don't like the way everything keeps coming back to the mummy. Everywhere you look, there's a connection. George died in its presence, Nicholas and Caroline died the same way as the Egyptians who discovered the tomb, and Rose kept going on about the curse. *Death shall come . . .*'

'You don't really believe in that sort of thing?' I said.

He met my gaze steadily. 'I've seen enough strange things in my time. I'm not ready to dismiss anything out of hand.'

'You have to draw the line somewhere,' I said.

'Do you?' said Stuart. 'These days, I don't care what the threat is. Just tell me how big a gun I need to deal with it.'

'Spoken like a typical ex-soldier,' I said, not unkindly.

'How much longer before Security get here?' said Chloe.

'Forty minutes,' said Stuart, not even glancing at the clock on the mantelpiece. 'Maybe longer.'

Marjorie heaved herself up out of her chair, and stood swaying on her feet. 'I need to go to the bathroom. And no, it can't wait.'

'Why didn't you go before we shut ourselves in here?' said Penny.

'Because I didn't need to before!' said Marjorie.

Bernard lurched to his feet. 'I need to visit the bathroom, too.'

'See what you've started!' said Penny.

Susan rose quickly to stand beside Bernard, and just like that we were all on our feet.

'I need the little girl's room!' Marjorie said loudly. 'Right now!'

'Damn!' said Penny. 'So do I, now.'

'All right!' I said.

'It's still a risk,' said Stuart.

'I need to piss!' said Marjorie.

'We should be safe enough, as long as we stick together,' I said. 'Pay attention, everyone! We're all going in one group, because I don't want to have to do this again. Chloe, where's the nearest bathroom?'

'Not far from here,' said Chloe. 'A few minutes, at most.'

'Then we go straight there,' said Stuart. 'We take care of the business and we come straight back. No diversions, no arguments, and no one goes off on their own.'

'You want to hold my hand while I'm in there?' said Marjorie.

I pulled the chair away, opened the door, and stepped outside. The corridor seemed still and peaceful enough.

'We should hurry,' said Susan, lowering her voice confidentially. 'I'm not sure how much longer Bernard can hold on.'

'It'll be quicker if I lead the way,' said Chloe.

'All right, fine!' said Marjorie. 'But can we please get moving? My bladder is so full my back teeth are floating.'

179

'Rather more information than I really needed,' murmured Penny.

I gave the corridor one more look, nodded to Chloe, and then stepped back out of her way. She strode off down the corridor, with Stuart at her side. Marjorie, Bernard and Susan followed quickly after her, leaving Penny and me to bring up the rear. And the hush of the house closed in around us.

Chloe set a good pace, while I chivvied everyone along from the rear. I felt we were all seriously exposed and vulnerable outside the drawing room. It was hard to look in every direction at once and still keep the group moving. They kept getting distracted, by sudden side turnings or exceptionally dark shadows, or some painted face glaring at them from the collection, but I drove them all on with loud reassurances and even louder bad language until Chloe finally brought us to the bathroom door.

I made everyone wait while I went in first to check it was safe. The white-tiled room was sparklingly clean, but only just large enough to hold the bare essentials. Toilet bowl, wash-basin, the usual amenities. And a pile of upmarket magazines in one corner, light reading for extended visits. People were going to have to queue, and there's nothing more vulnerable than a line of people whose minds are on other things. I came back out, indicated everything was fine, and Marjorie practically trampled me underfoot in her eagerness to be first. I had to close the door after her, because she had other things on her mind. And then I watched one end of the corridor, while Penny watched the other and Stuart kept everyone in line.

People went in and out, then stood around awkwardly, impatient to get back to the safety of the drawing room. Until I put my foot down, some were actually ready to go back on their own. The last thing I needed was people being picked off one by one, like Professor Rose. Stuart was the last one in, muttering under his breath about how long it was all taking. Penny looked at me.

'Just you, and then we're done.'

'No need,' I said. 'I can last for days, like a camel.'

'I really didn't need to know that,' said Penny.

I led the way back to the drawing room. Everyone seemed a little more relaxed now the pressure was off, and less inclined to jump at shadows. Until I stopped abruptly and glared about me.

'What is it?' said Stuart, looking quickly around. 'What's wrong?'

'Hush!' I said.

Bernard glared belligerently around him, his large hands clenched into fists. Susan clung on to his arm, as much to hold him back as for comfort. Chloe looked ready for anything, and Marjorie just looked even more fed up than usual. As though I'd only stopped to annoy her. Penny moved in beside me.

'What is it, Ishmael?'

'I can hear someone moving around,' I said quietly. 'Off in the distance, right at the edge of my hearing.'

181

Everyone listened, straining to hear anything in the silence.

'Are you hearing footsteps?' Stuart said finally. 'Like the ones we heard on the top floor?'

'What I'm hearing is definitely not soft or muffled,' I said firmly. 'Just ordinary human footsteps. Male, I'd say, from the weight and the stride. Except . . .'

'Oh, it's never good when you say that,' said Penny. 'Except what?'

'The rhythm is wrong,' I said, frowning. 'That isn't how people walk . . .'

They were all looking at me now, but none of them wanted to say anything. The corridor stretched away, open and empty, and the collection loomed around us.

'I really don't like us standing around,' Stuart said quietly. 'If we're not in any immediate danger, we should get moving again.'

'I really don't like the sound of those footsteps,' I said.

'Could it be the mummy?' said Penny.

I looked at her. 'If I offered you a large amount of money, would you stop saying that?'

'How large?' said Penny. And then her eyebrows rose sharply, as a thought struck her. 'Could someone be acting like a mummy to throw a scare into us?'

'Now that is more like it,' I said. I turned to Stuart. 'Get everyone back to the drawing room. Penny and I will check this out.'

Chloe looked at me sharply. 'You really think it's a good idea to go chasing off after footsteps only you can hear?'

'If I can track down the killer, the danger will be over,' I said.

'But can you do that?' said Marjorie.

'Yes,' said Stuart. 'He can. It's what he does.'

He nodded to me, and I nodded back. Two professionals who'd learned to trust each other's judgement and abilities. He gathered up the others and led them away. Penny waited till they'd all rounded the corner, and then looked at me steadily.

'I don't hear anything.'

'Neither do I, now,' I said. 'Whatever it was has moved out of range.'

'So where do we start looking?' said Penny.

'The last I heard, the footsteps were heading towards the mummy room,' I said. 'Where all of this began.'

'Where George was killed!' Penny shook her head. 'Wonderful!'

'Look on the bright side,' I said. 'Maybe the mummy will be back in its sarcophagus, and we can all relax a little.'

'The mood I'm in I'd haul the bloody thing out of the box, then rip it apart and dance on the pieces,' said Penny. 'Just on general principles.'

'Now you're talking.'

We moved quickly through the shadowy corridors, and the only footsteps were our own. We'd almost reached the door to the mummy room when I stopped abruptly again. Penny looked around quickly.

'Is someone here? I don't hear anything.'

'I'm smelling something,' I said. 'It's been hard

183

for me to smell anything useful in the fog of scents the collection gives off . . . but I'm picking up faint traces. Right here.'

'Traces of what?'

'Blood,' I said. 'I missed it before, because so much had been spilled in the mummy room.'

I turned my head slowly back and forth, breathing deeply, trying to isolate the scent . . . and then advanced on a length of shelving packed with Egyptian artefacts, crammed together in no particular order because they weren't that important. I thrust a hand into the midst of them and pulled out an object that had been pushed all the way to the back, out of sight. A heavy gold figurine some two foot tall, it was a stylized statue of a cat. Thickly encrusted with dried blood.

'The Egyptian goddess Bast,' I said. 'And the murder weapon. The killer used it to smash in George's head and then bludgeon him to death. There was no planning or preparation to George's murder, the killer just grabbed the nearest blunt instrument off the shelf.'

'So . . . not the mummy, after all!' said Penny.

'No,' I said. I studied the figurine carefully. 'Bast . . . symbol for the cunning of the cat and the rage of the lioness. The name has been translated as "devouring lady".'

'No wonder we didn't see it,' said Penny. 'Hidden away like that among all the other stuff . . .'

I looked at her sharply. 'Of course! That's it! Hidden in plain sight . . .'

I put the cat statue back on the shelf and raced back down the corridor. Penny quickly caught up with me.

184

'But . . . that's the murder weapon! Are you really going to just leave it there?'

'The killer doesn't know we know about it,' I said. 'It's safe enough.'

'Aren't we at least going to check out the mummy room?'

'The killer isn't in there,' I said. 'I would have heard him.'

'Then why are we running?'

'Because I've just realized where the missing mummy is.'

We ended up back in the entrance hall, taking in the sarcophagus standing against the wall beside the grandfather clock. Penny glared at the sarcophagus, fighting to get her breath back, and then glared at me.

'All right . . . it's still there. So what?'

'Do you remember Stuart telling us a story when we first arrived? This sarcophagus was originally occupied by an Ancient Egyptian called Nesmin, but the coffin was empty when the Cardavans acquired it. An unoccupied box, just like the one you hid in at the British Museum.'

Penny grinned suddenly, as I levered the lid off the sarcophagus and leaned it against the grandfather clock. And there, inside the coffin, was the shrivelled-up figure George had shown us earlier. The mummy was just as dead as before, but the whole of its chest had been smashed in. The edges of the hole were ragged, the bandages torn and tattered. The chest cavity showed traces of ancient packing materials, to hold something in place that wasn't there any longer.

'Looks like someone ripped the heart right out of her,' said Penny, wrinkling her nose as she leaned in for a closer look.

'Not the heart,' I said. 'That would have been removed before the embalming process began, along with all the other inner organs, so they could be stored in separate jars. Something was concealed inside this mummy a very long time ago. And now our elusive thief has it.'

'Some kind of treasure?' said Penny.

'Historical treasure,' I said. 'Of extraordinary value. And the only person in this house with the background and knowledge to know where to find it was Professor Rose. But it would have taken enormous strength to do this much damage . . . I would have thought something like this was beyond him.'

'No!' said Penny, bouncing up and down excitedly. 'I get it now! This is why the professor was abducted . . . Because he knew about the mummy. The killer took the professor away to interrogate him!'

'OK,' I said. 'That makes sense.'

'Then why are you pulling that face?'

'Because the odds are Rose is dead now. The killer wouldn't need him once he'd talked.'

'But you already thought he was dead.'

'I suspected it, but I hoped otherwise. As long as he was just missing, there was still a chance I could find him. And save him.' I looked at the shrivelled-up thing leaning awkwardly in its new resting place. It was too small for such a large box, like a child dumped in an adult coffin. 'There never was a mummy reanimated by an ancient curse. It was all just misdirection. Sorry to disappoint you, Penny.'

She shrugged briskly. 'I never liked the look of it. Nothing like a proper movie mummy. So what do we do now?'

I lifted the coffin lid off the grandfather clock and placed it back on the sarcophagus, shutting the mummy in again.

'We go back to the drawing room,' I said. 'Because if the mummy never walked and Professor Rose is dead . . .'

'Then one of the people in the drawing room has to be the killer,' said Penny.

'Looks like it,' I said. 'Which means every person in that room but one is in mortal danger.'

We ran all the way back. Penny had to struggle to keep up, wheezing like a steam engine with a leak in its boiler, but she hung on in there. I ran straight up to the closed drawing-room door and beat on it with my fist, while Penny staggered to a halt, leaned on the wall, and made really unpleasant noises. Glaring at me because I wasn't even out of breath. I beat on the door again.

'Open up! This is Ishmael, and Penny. I finally know what's going on!'

The door opened and I forced my way in, with Penny right behind me. Stuart made a point of closing the door and wedging the chair back in place, before going over to stand with Chloe. I started to explain, and then stopped as I looked at Stuart and Chloe, Bernard and Susan. They all looked seriously upset.

'What is it?' said Penny. 'What's happened?'

187

'Where's Marjorie?' I said.

'She went missing on the way back,' Stuart said harshly. 'Disappeared when I wasn't looking, just like Professor Rose. None of us noticed anything.'

Penny looked at me. 'How . . .?'

'Never mind the how,' I said. 'Stick to the why. Why would the killer want Marjorie? What could she know that the killer needs to know?'

'What are you talking about?' said Chloe.

'Later,' I said. 'We have to find Marjorie while there's a chance she might still be alive. The rest of you, stay here. And don't open the door again till we come back. If you get caught short again, use a flower vase.'

'How long are you planning to be gone?' said Chloe.

'As long as it takes,' I said.

Seven
A Matter of Death and Life

Outside the drawing room, surrounded by shadows and silence, I took a good look down the long corridor, while Penny waited patiently. There was nothing to see: just shelves of artefacts, the odd piece of expensive if not particularly attractive furniture, and the occasional painting of someone who almost certainly wasn't an ancestor of anyone currently living in Cardavan House. Nowhere our elusive killer could be hiding, no locked doors or intriguing side passages, and nothing even a little bit mysterious. And yet . . . I didn't trust any of it. Penny shifted from one foot to the other.

'I know,' I said, not looking round. 'It's just . . . I've got a bad feeling about this. Like the quiet before the storm, or the false sense of security you get in an open clearing . . . just before the big cat jumps out at you from ambush.'

'What are you so nervous about?' said Penny. 'At best it's a mummy, at worst it's a serial killer. We can handle either of those without even breaking into a sweat.'

'Normally I'd agree with you,' I said. 'Normally I'd be striding down this corridor shouting "Come on, give me your best shot!", but something feels wrong. Like we're facing something seriously out of the ordinary, even for us.'

'Concentrate on the matter in hand,' Penny said wisely. 'Starting with why would anyone want to abduct Marjorie. She doesn't know anything important about the collection, like Professor Rose, so what would the killer want with her?'

'This can't be about the collection,' I said. 'Marjorie didn't give a damn about any of it. But she might know George's security codes, or where he hid his off-the-books business records. Maybe there is some connection between the killings and George's security work, after all . . .'

'I was so sure someone in the drawing room was the killer,' said Penny. 'But if Marjorie has been carried off by force, then there must be someone else in the house.'

'Not necessarily,' I said. 'We have no proof Marjorie was abducted. She could have just sneaked away on her own, for reasons of her own.'

'Hold everything! Go previous and slam on the brakes,' said Penny. 'Are you suggesting Marjorie might be the killer? You saw the state of her! If she was any more drunk she'd be sweating rubbing alcohol!'

'She could have been faking it,' I said patiently, 'To give her an excuse to leave the drawing room. She couldn't have known everyone else would insist on going to the bathroom with her.'

'But what reason could Marjorie possibly have for killing so many people?' said Penny. 'George, Nicholas, Caroline, Professor Rose . . .?'

'With George dead, Marjorie inherits everything,' I said. 'As for the others, maybe it's just more misdirection. Kill four people, so one won't stand out . . . No, that doesn't work. The extreme manner of George's death is enough to make him stand out anyway. I think it's all about whatever was hidden inside the mummy. Once we find out what that is, then we'll know why so many people had to die because of it.'

'But in the meantime Marjorie is still missing,' said Penny. 'And possibly in danger of her life. What are we going to do, Ishmael?'

'Find her,' I said. 'And then either rescue her or pin her to the wall and ask her a whole bunch of pertinent questions.'

'What if there's more to it than that?' said Penny.

I looked down the corridor, and the darkness and the hush looked back at me.

'Wouldn't surprise me in the least.'

We both looked round quickly as the drawing room door opened, and Stuart came out. He closed the door firmly behind him, looked suspiciously down the corridor and then turned to us. His face was set in harsh, unforgiving lines, and his eyes were angry. It took me a moment to realize he was angry at himself, for letting another of the people in his care disappear without trace. He settled into his usual parade rest stance and started talking in a low, steady voice. There was something of the confessional in his manner, as though he felt the need to justify himself.

'I never heard a thing. Marjorie just vanished while my back was turned. She was so drunk she had trouble keeping up, and I was so busy leading from the front I never thought to look back. I didn't hear her leave, and I definitely didn't hear her being abducted. I didn't hear any strange footsteps, before or afterwards. Nothing to suggest there was anyone else in the corridor.'

I believed him. Old soldiers have good instincts for what's going on around them in the field. It's what keeps them alive.

'Don't beat yourself up,' I said. 'No one else heard anything either. Whoever's doing this is good. Really good.'

'But I was in charge,' said Stuart. 'They were my responsibility.'

'We were wondering if Marjorie might have gone off on her own,' Penny said carefully. 'Because she had business of her own to attend to.'

Stuart nodded slowly. 'I did wonder that about Professor Rose. Whether the reason why I did not hear him being taken was because no one took him. But why would either of them go wandering off on their own in such a dangerous situation?'

'People will risk anything,' I said, 'if the payout is big enough.'

Stuart looked at me sharply. 'What payout? What are you talking about? Do you know something I don't?'

'Most of the time,' I said.

'Ishmael . . .' murmured Penny. 'Play nicely with the nice Colonel.'

'Penny and I could be gone for a while,' I said to Stuart, in a tone that was almost an apology. 'So once you go back in, keep that door shut whatever happens. And protect the others.'

'Whatever it takes,' said Stuart. For a moment he looked every inch the soldier he still was when it mattered, ready to fight to the last drop of the enemy's blood. He nodded briskly to us, went back inside, and shut the door. I waited till I heard the chair being jammed firmly into place, and then turned to Penny.

'I thought he'd never go . . .' I said lightly.

'How are we supposed to find Marjorie in a house this size,' said Penny, determined not to be sidetracked, 'given that we've already checked every room and passageway and shadowy corner in this dump once, looking for Professor Rose, and couldn't find him anywhere?'

'Marjorie has one advantage over the professor,' I said. 'Namely, a strong and highly distinctive perfume. I noticed it the moment I met her. Hell, it was so strong it reached out, slapped me round the face and brought tears to my eyes. All we have to do is go back to the bathroom and follow the route they took back, and I can use her perfume to figure out exactly where she left the group.'

'And, of course, you remember the route . . .' said Penny.

'Of course,' I said.

'You get on my nerves sometimes! You know that?' said Penny. 'Can you really track her by her perfume in a house full of Ancient Egyptian smells?'

'It's not going to be easy,' I said. 'But given the perfume nearly took my head off at close quarters, it should be like following a trail of really smelly breadcrumbs.'

'Oh, ick!' said Penny.

Penny stuck close beside me as we made our way through the house, keeping a careful eye on every

193

door and side turning we passed. Neither of us trusted the house an inch. Our footsteps sounded loud and carried clearly on the wooden floorboards. I couldn't hear anything else. Faint traces of Marjorie's scent bobbed along on the air before me, like telltale bubbles rising up out of the swamp of smells.

'Do you have any idea what might have been hidden inside the mummy?' said Penny, after a while. There's nothing like unending quiet and unbearable pressure to make people want to break the silence and defy the tension with the sound of their own voice. 'I mean, why would anyone go to such lengths to conceal something inside a mummy, inside a sarcophagus, inside a tomb?'

'Remember the story Professor Rose told us?' I said. 'About the magical gem that fell from the heavens. Cleopatra used it to make herself unnaturally powerful and kill off her enemies by sucking the life out of them.'

'Rose said the gem was lost,' said Penny. 'Which was why Cleopatra fell from power.'

'But was it lost? Or was it stolen from her?' I said. 'As a result of some conspiracy among her own people because she'd become too powerful? And maybe they hid it inside her mummified body, because that was the perfect ironic hiding place . . . for something none of them wanted around any more.'

'Why not take it for themselves?' said Penny. 'Why weren't they tempted to become powerful and immortal?'

'I don't think they trusted it, or each other, after seeing what the gem did to Cleopatra,'

194

I said. 'So they got rid of it permanently. A group decision, for the good of all.'

'An Ancient Egyptian jewel with that kind of legend attached would be a real prize for any collector,' said Penny. 'And more than enough to attract a top-rank professional thief. No wonder they've been running rings round us.'

'It still doesn't explain why George was bludgeoned to death, while the others died without a mark on them,' I said. 'We're missing some vital piece of information . . . that will make everything fall into place once we have it. And the best way to find that information is to find the thief and make them tell us.'

'After we save Marjorie,' said Penny, just a bit pointedly.

'If she needs saving,' I said, just as pointedly. 'She could have heard the story from Professor Rose long before the rest of us. She's had plenty of time to be tempted and make plans.'

'But she was going to inherit the whole collection anyway,' said Penny. 'Including the mummy. All she had to do was wait.'

'Everyone said Marjorie was a gold-digger,' I said. 'Perhaps she'd just had enough of George and the collection.'

'So all that drunken stuff about her lovely George . . . None of that was true?'

'Unfortunately,' I said, 'people sometimes really are just what they appear to be.'

It didn't take long to find where Marjorie left the group. Halfway down the corridor from the bathroom. Someone hadn't wasted any time . . .

I followed her scent down a side passageway, breathing deeply so as not to lose the trail. Heavier scents from the collection filled my head like the clamour of an excited crowd, but Marjorie's perfume rose above them through sheer impact. And then something caught my attention, and I slowed my pace right down. Penny looked at me inquiringly and I gestured for her to lean in close.

'What is it?' she whispered. 'Have you lost the trail?'

'We're not alone,' I said. 'The footsteps are back.'

Penny glanced casually back the way we'd come. 'I don't see anyone.'

'They're keeping well back,' I said. 'Carry on as though we haven't noticed, but keep it down to an amble. Let's see if we can tempt the killer into catching up with us.'

'And then?'

'Then I grab him, shake him hard till his eyes change colour, and get some answers out of him.'

'Sounds like a plan to me,' said Penny.

We strolled down the corridor, giving our stalker every opportunity to catch up with us, but the footsteps kept their distance. And once again that strange inner alarm was sounding in my head. Like a cold iron bell in the middle of a forest at midnight. A voice from out of my past, warning me urgently to beware of something.

'When you heard those footsteps before,' Penny murmured, 'you said they sounded wrong. Has that changed?'

'No,' I said. 'Though I'm still having a hard

196

time putting my finger on exactly what it is that's wrong. It's just . . . people don't walk like that.'

'If it's not people,' Penny said carefully, 'does that mean . . . not human?'

'No. It's still a man.'

'You're not being very helpful.'

'I know!'

'We can safely assume they aren't Marjorie's footsteps?' said Penny.

'Definitely,' I said. 'I've heard Marjorie walk. This is nothing like her.'

'Then there is someone else in the house!'

'I don't know,' I said. 'I've had to change my mind so many times my brain has whiplash. Keep going. I'm still following the perfume.'

'Are you smelling any blood?'

'No,' I said. 'But that doesn't mean as much as it used to.'

I rounded a corner and there was George's study. The perfume trail stopped right outside the closed door. I stopped and looked at the door. Penny looked at it, and then at me.

'Is this it?'

'Yes,' I said. 'She went in there. Into George's study.'

'That has to mean something,' said Penny.

'Yes,' I said. 'But don't ask me what.'

'Are you picking up any other scents? People scents?'

'All I'm getting is the perfume,' I said. 'Given how easy a trail it was to follow, I'm starting to wonder if we were brought here deliberately and Marjorie is just bait in a trap. For example, look at the door.'

'What about it?' said Penny.

'It was standing open when Stuart and I left,' I said. 'So why is it closed now? What don't they want us to see?'

'Why bring Marjorie here, anyway?' said Penny.

'Good question,' I said. I pressed my ear against the wood of the door. 'I'm not hearing anything inside the room.'

'What about the footsteps?' said Penny, glancing back the way we'd come.

I straightened up, still looking at the door. 'They've stopped. I think the killer has us right where he wants us.'

'Are you about to say it's too quiet?'

'I wouldn't dare.'

'Marjorie could be tied up and gagged in there.'

'Let's hope so.'

'Ishmael!' Penny looked at me, shocked. 'That's an awful thing to say.'

'If she isn't,' I said steadily, 'then the odds are she's dead. Because she should have heard us by now and she hasn't called out for help.'

I opened the door and strode into George's study, with Penny all but treading on my heels. Marjorie was sitting behind George's desk. There wasn't a mark on her, and her eyes were closed. She could almost have been sleeping. I closed the door, to make sure we wouldn't be interrupted, and then moved behind the desk to check Marjorie's vital signs. Just in case. I looked back at Penny and shook my head.

'Damn!' said Penny. 'I was just starting to like her. Did she die the same way as Nicholas and Caroline?'

'Looks like it,' I said. 'But don't ask me how.'

'So she wasn't the killer,' said Penny. 'Maybe what she said about George was true, after all.'

'Probably,' I said kindly.

'But why bring her here to kill her? It's not much of a hiding place.'

'The killer doesn't seem to care where we find his kills,' I said. I took a quick look around the study. 'Nothing has been moved since I was last here. So presumably the killer wasn't interested in George's work, nor the security aspects. This was just the first room the killer came to where he could kill Marjorie without being heard by the others.'

'So he had no interest in interrogating her?' said Penny. 'He only ever wanted to kill her?'

'Bait in a trap,' I said. 'To lure us here.'

'Whoever it is, they must be really strong,' said Penny. 'Marjorie wouldn't have gone quietly. She'd have fought like hell.'

I suddenly looked round at the closed door. 'The footsteps are coming down the corridor towards us.'

Penny moved beside me and we stood together facing the door. The alarm in my head shrieked desperately, like a wounded animal trying to warn the rest of its pack. Something bad was coming. And something deep inside me told me I knew what it was, if I would only remember . . .

The footsteps grew steadily louder as they approached the door, and Penny's head came up as she heard them too. They sounded soft and oddly muffled, and something in the way the killer walked jarred painfully against my sensibilities.

People weren't supposed to walk like that. The footsteps finally came to a halt on the other side of the door. I waited, but nothing happened. My muscles ached with the strain of standing so still. Penny clutched at my arm.

'What's he doing out there?' she murmured.

'Standing still,' I said quietly. 'I can hear him breathing. I think . . . he's listening to us listening to him.'

I was tempted to yank open the door and strike down whoever was out there with all my strength. Kill the killer, so we could all be safe. And so I'd never have to feel this way again. Because he scared me, for reasons I couldn't understand . . . But I couldn't kill him while I still had questions only he could answer.

Penny must have seen something in my face. 'What's wrong, Ishmael? You can take him.'

'Can I?' I said, not looking away from the closed door. 'How can I be sure when I don't know what's out there? I have no idea what it is, or what it wants.'

'It?' said Penny.

'It doesn't walk like a man,' I said.

'At least we can be sure it's not the mummy,' said Penny.

I managed a small smile. 'There is that, yes. Go stand by the far wall, Penny. I think I'm going to need room to manoeuvre in order to handle this.'

I waited till Penny had retreated the whole distance of the room, then took a deep breath and hauled open the door. I grabbed the arm of the man waiting outside and jerked him inside.

It was Professor Rose. I threw him to the floor and slammed the door shut. Rose hit the floor hard, but in a moment was up on his feet again facing me. He didn't stand like a man: he crouched like an animal at bay, or a predator poised to strike. His balance was wrong, as though something inside him had broken or shifted. I was between him and the only exit, but he didn't even glance at the door. Or at Penny, or the dead woman sitting behind the desk. He didn't care about them. He only had eyes for me.

Professor Rose smiled slowly. A vicious, dangerous strangely triumphant smile. I gave him my best cold stare, and he met my gaze unflinchingly with unblinking eyes. The smile stretched his mouth unnaturally, till I was surprised it didn't split his cheeks. It must have been painful, but he didn't seem to care. I looked him over carefully. I'd given him up for dead so many times it was almost a shock to see him alive. All those theories I'd come up with, and now it was him! It didn't make sense . . . Except Rose knew all there was to know about the story of Cleopatra's gem, so who better to find and take it? He didn't look like a thief or a killer. He just looked . . . wrong. Not the quiet unassuming historian who'd jousted with me over our respective scholarly reputations. The figure before me was like something out of a nightmare. Spiritually twisted and distorted, trembling with barely suppressed energies . . .

Ready to fight or run, or do something awful. Just because he could.

'You're not wearing any shoes,' I said. With

so much strangeness in the room, it was a relief to concentrate on something I did understand. Something that finally made sense. 'You've been walking around in your socks. That's why your footsteps sounded so soft and muffled! Especially on the carpeted floor upstairs. All to make us think the mummy was up and about. But even so, how did you freak those people out so completely?'

Rose didn't answer. He just crouched before me, staring at me, smiling his inhuman smile.

'It was the way you walked,' I said. 'The stance was wrong and the rhythms, and the way you carried your weight . . . Enough to affect everyone on a subconscious level, even if they didn't know why. How much of this was planned, Professor? Wanting to sound like a mummy to confuse the issue . . . yes, I get that but how much was down to the fact that you just couldn't walk like a man any more? What have you done to yourself?'

'Don't you know?' said Rose. His voice was harsh and the inflections were all wrong. He didn't sound like Rose at all.

'I know you're the killer,' I said. 'I know you took something out of the mummy. But why? What's this all about?'

'It's a matter of death and life,' said Rose. 'You should know that.'

'I really don't,' I said. 'None of this makes any sense.'

Rose cocked his head slightly to one side, as if to see me more clearly. 'Then let me make things clear to you.'

He went for me, surging forward impossibly fast. His outstretched hands reached for my throat, the fingers curved into claws. I grabbed hold of his wrists with both hands and brought him to a sudden halt. His wrists felt hard as iron, hot as coals, as though he was burning up from the inside. I held him off, but only just. He threw all his strength against me, and it took all my more than human strength to stop him. No wonder the others died so easily; they wouldn't have stood a chance against something like this. No one would. Rose pressed forward inch by inch, straining so hard his whole body trembled.

I fell back, trying to catch him off balance and throw him to one side, but he matched my every move. We staggered back and forth across the study, crashing against the furniture and trampling over the wreckage. We surged this way and that, our eyes locked on each other. Rose's smile never wavered. He fought to get to me, and I fought to hold him off. And nothing else mattered.

Penny had the good sense to stay out of the way, pressed up against the far wall. She knew there was nothing she could do to help.

Rose pushed forward despite everything I could do. I didn't dare let go of his wrists to hit him. And I wasn't sure I could hurt him, anyway. His whole body shuddered with the effort of what he was doing, and his wrists were so hot they almost burned my hands. Rose was calling on all his resources, burning himself up just to get to me. As though it didn't matter to him whether he lived or died.

The alarm screamed in my head like a dying thing.

And then Rose's hands leapt forward, and I didn't have enough strength left to stop him. But he didn't go for my throat. Instead, his hands fastened on to both sides of my head. I cried in pain at the terrible pressure, as his hands closed like a vice. Rose stared unblinkingly into my eyes, his smile so wide now it was a wonder the skin didn't split open to reveal the teeth beneath. We stood face to face, both of us flushed and panting from our exertions. I tightened my grip on his wrists and felt the bones crack and break, but Rose didn't flinch and his grip on my head didn't weaken.

A sudden glow blazed in Rose's eyes, and strange energies leapt out to hit me full in the face. It was like staring into the sun, a force so terrible it was capable of burning me up in a moment. But I wouldn't look away. And then it was like standing before a black hole, a weird inhuman vortex sucking everything into itself. And suddenly I understood, Rose wanted my life energies so he could feast on them . . . Except I wouldn't let them go. I clamped down hard, clinging on to my life with everything I had. Rose cried out in frustration, the terrible light in his eyes snapped off, and all the strength went out of him. He collapsed bonelessly, falling to his knees, only held up by my grip on his wrists.

There was another presence in the room now. Something wild and powerful, invisible and utterly inhuman. Like a ghost gone bad, or a god brought low. It hung on the air, seething and crackling, and then shot off through the doorway and was gone. I could feel it howling down the corridor in search of new prey. I slowly opened my hands, letting go of Professor Rose's wrists. He fell to the floor, and didn't move.

I was trembling all over. I had looked death in the eye and defied it. And felt tired, so tired. Penny came forward tentatively, and then stopped as she saw the look on my face.

'Did you see that?' I asked harshly.

'See what, Ishmael?'

'Didn't you feel it?'

'Feel what? I don't understand, Ishmael. What just happened here? And what's wrong with Professor Rose?'

She really didn't know what I was talking about. She hadn't been able to see or sense the terrible thing that had hidden inside Rose, like the gem in the mummy. I reached out to Penny, still trembling, and she took me in her arms and held me tightly. After a while I let go of her, and she immediately let go of me. She knew I could only bear to be weak for so long. I looked down at Rose, curled up in a ball on the floor, barely breathing. I knelt down beside him and checked his pulse. It was weak and thready, growing fainter by the moment. Penny knelt down, looking worriedly at me rather than the professor.

'What's wrong with him, Ishmael?'

'He's dying,' I said. 'He's all used up.'

'Isn't there anything you can do to help him?'

'No. He's been emptied out, from inside.'

Rose slowly opened his eyes to look at me. And when he spoke, forcing the words out with one last effort, he sounded like himself again.

'It wasn't me. None of it was me.'

'I know,' I said.

'Something got inside me. The *ka* . . .'

He stopped breathing. His whole body fell in upon itself, shaking and shuddering, withering away until he resembled nothing so much as the mummy he'd studied for so long. The thing inside him had used up all his energies to fuel its fight with me. I started to get to my feet, and almost collapsed. I was trembling again, from the narrowness of my escape. Penny had to help me up.

'Why did the professor want to kill you?' she asked quietly.

'It was more than that.' I fought to keep my voice calm. 'Something inside him tried to suck the life out of me.'

Her eyes widened. 'Like a vampire?'

'Something like that, I suppose.' I had to be careful what I said. Penny had good reason to be terrified of vampires. 'Whatever it was, it couldn't take my life the way it did with Nicholas, Caroline and Marjorie. Because they were human, while I . . . have other resources. If I hadn't beaten this thing, it would have left Rose and got inside me. Walked around the house in my body, doing awful things with my strength.'

'So Rose was the killer all along?' said Penny.

'People died because of him,' I said carefully. 'He sucked the life out of Nicholas and Caroline and Marjorie – that's why there wasn't a mark on them to show how they died. He got to them because they never saw the professor as a threat. But George . . . I still don't understand what happened to George. That was a completely

206

different kind of death. Whatever had got inside Rose was strong enough to have beaten George that badly, but why would it want to?'

'Because George stole the mummy and had it brought here?'

'No. I think it wanted to come here. Remember the dreams that led the locals to uncover Cleopatra's tomb? Something dreamed those dreams for them.'

'Rose said there was something inside him,' said Penny. 'That something got in . . .'

'It's not here any more,' I said. 'I felt it leave.'

'But what is it? What's going on, Ishmael? Talk to me!'

I looked round the office, found two chairs and stood them up, and gestured for Penny to sit down facing me. She did so, reluctantly, and I did my best to sound calm and reasonable while I talked of impossible things.

'It all goes back to Ancient Egypt,' I said. 'The story Professor Rose told us of an amazing magical gem that fell from the heavens.'

'You don't believe in magical gems,' said Penny.

'No, I don't. But I have good reason to believe that strange and powerful things sometimes fall from the skies.'

'You think the gem was something alien?'

'Some kind of misunderstood alien tech,' I said. 'Or possibly something alive . . . Cleopatra used it to suck the life out of her enemies to make herself strong. That's why the people around her took it away from her. Because they knew what a danger it was to all of them. Without the gem to keep her going, Cleopatra died. And they hid the thing inside her mummified body and sealed them both in the tomb forever. They even wiped the first Cleopatra's name from history, so no one would look for her or the thing inside her. And there the gem stayed for more than two thousand years. Dreaming in the dark, waiting for a chance to live again . . .

'Rose must have found a more complete version of the story, that told him where to look. Or perhaps the gem called to him. Either way, he opened up the mummy and took the thing for himself. Perhaps because he just couldn't stand the thought of someone like George having it. And then the gem took him . . . Rose's last word was "*ka*". We talked about that earlier. The Ancient Egyptian idea of a soul that could exist separately from its body. Which was sometimes so strong it could over-power a weaker soul and force it out. Rose found the gem, and it woke up. And it woke up hungry.'

'The gem, or something in it, possessed Rose?' said Penny.

'It took control of him, and then ate him up from the inside. Sent him creeping round the house to make itself stronger by stealing the life energies from others. That's why Rose disap-peared. So he could prey on his victims one at a time, because he wasn't strong enough to take on the whole group.'

'When do you think all this started?' said Penny. 'When was Rose first possessed? How long has something else been living in his body, watching us through his eyes and getting ready to make its first move?'

'I don't know,' I said. 'It's possible we never met the real Professor Rose until just now.'

'So everything that's happened in this house is the result of an ancient curse, after all?' said Penny.

'It's starting to look that way,' I said. 'But why does this thing need to take so many lives? Why not just hide inside someone until it can figure out a way to get home again?'

'It's planning something,' said Penny.

'Seems likely,' I said. I rose to my feet and Penny got up to face me. 'Come on. We need to get back to the others. Because this isn't over yet.'

Eight
Questions and Answers

I started for the door and then stopped, as I realized Penny was making no move to follow me. She stood beside the desk, looking at Marjorie sitting slumped in her chair. I could see Penny was troubled, but I didn't understand why. She'd seen worse, in cases we'd handled before. In our line of work, bad situations come with the territory. Penny suddenly turned to look at me. And just like that, I wanted to look away. Because I knew what questions she was going to ask, and the only answers I had weren't going to make her feel any better.

'She looks so peaceful,' said Penny. 'But Marjorie wasn't just killed, she had the life torn out of her to feed something alien. Talk to me, Ishmael. I need to understand this.'

'Ask me anything,' I said. Because she was my partner, and I could only protect her from the things she allowed me to.

'The alien hiding inside Professor Rose sucked out Marjorie's life energies,' said Penny. 'But did it also eat her soul?'

'I don't think so,' I said. 'It feeds on the energies, that's all. It takes control of a body by pushing that body's *ka* to one side, but the original person is still in there. Remember how Professor

210

Rose spoke to us at the end? Once the possessor left Rose's body, he was himself again.'

Penny nodded slowly, accepting what I had to say; for the moment. For which I was grateful. I wasn't lying, as far as I knew. My explanation made sense, it fitted all the facts . . . But did I believe it because I wanted it to be true? Because the alternative was simply too horrifying to bear? Not just an energy vampire, but an eater of souls . . .

Who seemed to know me. Who hated me, because of someone I didn't even remember being.

'Do we have to leave Marjorie's body here?' Penny said finally. 'And the professor's?'

'We've already been through this,' I said patiently. 'With Nicholas and Caroline. What good would it do to move them? They're beyond our help. The bodies will be safe and secure here, and that's all we can do for them right now.'

'It still doesn't feel right,' said Penny. 'We failed them, Ishmael, and now it feels like we're abandoning them.'

'We have to concentrate on the living,' I said. 'On saving those we can save.'

'We're not doing very well with that, are we?' said Penny. 'We came here to protect people, but the bodies just keep piling up.'

'We can only do what we can,' I said. 'At least now we know what we're up against.'

'Do we?' said Penny. Her eyes flashed angrily and she stepped away from the desk to confront me. 'It's a magical gem, or a piece of alien tech . . . Something that hid inside a mummy for thousands of years. And now it's hiding inside people so it can suck the life out of others.' She

211

stopped, and looked at me for a long moment. As though she wasn't sure who she was looking at. 'It knew you, Ishmael. That thing knew who and what you really are . . .'

'You know I have no memories of what I was before I was me,' I said steadily. 'If I ever knew anything about this alien vampire thing, I don't know now.'

'Why didn't it eat you?' said Penny.

'Because it couldn't,' I said. 'Maybe my body is human but my energies aren't. Perhaps we're just not compatible.'

I looked at her hopefully, searching for even a small smile, but there was nothing. I couldn't reach her. I gestured at the open door.

'We have to go, Penny. It's still out there, somewhere. We can't just stand around talking while people are in danger.'

'You're right,' said Penny. 'We'll talk as we go.'

I led the way back through the house. Penny strode along beside me, not talking, thinking her own thoughts. We'd spent so long searching for answers, trying to understand what was happening . . . And now we knew, we were no happier. The shadows all around us were as deep and dark as ever, but they didn't bother me any more. Because I'd met the monster and it was darker than any shadow could ever be.

'What do you think the *ka* thief will do now?' said Penny.

'*Ka* thief?' I said. 'That's what we're calling it?'

'Do you have a better name?'

'Not yet, but give me a while . . .'

212

'What will the *ka* thief do, now it knows we know what it is?' said Penny, determined to stick to the point and not be distracted.

'It will hide inside someone else,' I said. 'So it can use their body. It needs a physical form to have a physical effect on others. It didn't even try to drain me until it had both its hands in place on my head.'

'Why does it need to do that?' said Penny.

'Beats the hell out of me,' I said. 'Maybe it's like completing a circuit . . .'

I did my best to keep my voice light, but the memory of what the alien thing had tried to do made me shudder. Penny put a comforting hand on my arm, just for a moment. We moved on through the corridors in silence.

'At least the security people will be here soon,' Penny said finally. 'We only have to hold the *ka* thief off for a while.'

'No,' I said immediately. 'More people arriving means more people for the *ka* thief to feed on to make it stronger. We have to put a stop to this thing before Security get here. It wants to be the last man standing, the only survivor, free to tell Security whatever story it wants to and then leave the house with them. It wants to get out and turn the whole world into one big feeding ground. Maybe it'll latch on to another Cleopatra, another person in power, and take charge again. There's more than one way to drain the life out of humanity, slower and better ways to make them suffer. Whatever this alien thing is, it doesn't just hate me; it hates everything that isn't it. Whatever happens, we can't allow the *ka* thief to leave this house.'

'You want to kill it?' said Penny.

'Of course,' I said. 'Do you have a problem with that?'

'After everything it's done? No. But . . . it could have answers to all the questions of your life. Who you really are, where you came from. If you kill it, you might never learn the truth.'

'I can live with that,' I said.

Penny nodded slowly, as though that was the answer she'd been hoping for.

'Did you think I'd be tempted to keep it alive?' I said. 'I'm human because I choose to be, and I will protect humanity from everything that threatens it. Even my own temptation.'

'Of course you will,' said Penny. And she smiled at me for the first time since we discovered the truth about Professor Rose.

'The team's back together again,' I said solemnly.

'How do you kill something that doesn't have a body?' said Penny. 'If we kill the body it's possessing, won't it just jump to another host?'

'I don't know,' I said. 'Maybe if we knock it unconscious and keep it that way until we figure out some way to get the alien out and then kill it . . .'

'You really think that will work?'

'Beats the hell out of me,' I said.

We finally came to the long corridor that led to the drawing room. All the way there I'd been listening carefully for the alarm in my head, but there was nothing. As though it only existed to send a warning, and now I knew what the threat was the alarm had shut itself down. It bothered

214

me that I hadn't even known it was there. I had
to wonder what else from my previous existence
I might have hidden away inside me.

Sometimes I wonder if the old me is caged
deep inside, waiting for the bars of the cage to
weaken so it can get out. Sometimes I wonder if
I'm just the smile on the face of the tiger . . .
And sometimes I think it's hard enough to be
human, without worrying about anything else.

I suddenly realized the door to the drawing
room was standing open. I concentrated, and
heard raised angry voices inside the room. I
sprinted down the corridor and burst through the
open door to find Bernard and Stuart standing
toe to toe, shouting into each other's faces.
Bernard was almost apoplectic with rage, and
even more confused than normal. He didn't seem
too sure who Stuart was, but that didn't stop him
brandishing a fist in his face while ranting and
raving at the top of his voice. Stuart had to shout
back just to make himself heard. He was trying
to get through to Bernard to calm him down, but
Bernard wasn't listening.

'I want Susan!' he roared, his face dangerously
flushed. 'I'm not staying here with you, I want my
wife! Get out of my way or I'll knock you down.
I'm going to get her and you can't stop me!'

Stuart stood his ground. Bernard gave him a
good hard shove in the chest, but Stuart didn't
move. Bernard went to go round him, and Stuart
grabbed him by the arm. Bernard attacked him,
lashing out with both fists. He was almost sobbing
with rage and frustration, but his blows had real
strength and speed. Stuart did his best to fend

Bernard off without hurting him, deflecting most of the punches with raised arms, but some still got through. The sound of Bernard's fists striking home on Stuart's face was flat and vicious, but Stuart didn't flinch or cry out. He just held his ground and did his best to contain the old man's fury. He was the Colonel, a trained soldier who'd seen action in dangerous places. He could have taken Bernard down in a dozen different ways, but he didn't. Because he didn't want to hurt his wife's grandfather.

I grabbed Bernard from behind and dragged him away from Stuart. I pinned his arms to his sides in a bear hug so he couldn't lash out, but he still fought me, shouting incoherently. Fortunately, his strength was no match for mine. Penny arrived just in time to see me dump him back in his usual chair, with enough force to knock the breath out of him. It was a relief not to listen to him shouting any more.

Penny hurried forward to speak soothingly to Bernard and her female voice got through to him, although Stuart and I couldn't. He quickly calmed down, already forgetting why he'd been so angry. 'Susan,' he kept saying. 'I want Susan.' Not like a man missing his wife, but a child who wanted his mother.

I left Penny talking to him, and took Stuart off to one side. He had a handkerchief pressed to one nostril, mopping up some blood, and the beginnings of a truly impressive black eye. But neither of them made any impression on his usual calm and unruffled demeanour. He tugged at his jacket here and there to make sure it was hanging properly, because the proper form must always be observed when you're officer material.

'Thanks for the help,' he said gruffly. 'I thought I could handle him, but Bernard in a raging fury is a lot stronger than he has any right to be. His mind may be failing him, but his body hasn't. The man's as strong as an ox. And almost as easy to reason with.' He checked his handkerchief, put it away, straightened his cuffs, and then looked at me thoughtfully. 'How were you able to handle him so easily?'

'It's all in the training,' I said. 'Why did you open the door? Where are Susan and Chloe?'

Stuart scowled. 'Bernard made a fuss about wanting something from his rooms on the top floor. Some favourite cigar case that he'd forgotten to transfer from his jacket pocket when he changed for dinner. He kept saying he was going to go and get it, and wouldn't listen to any of us when we said it wasn't safe. In the end Susan said she'd go in his place, because he'd only get lost on the way or forget where he was supposed to come back to. She wouldn't be talked out of it, either. Apparently Bernard has a tendency to obsess over certain familiar objects until they're all that can settle him down. I suppose when you can't depend on your memories any more, things become more important because they bring memories with them.

'Susan had to go because she was the only one who knew where to look for the cigar case. Chloe and I both volunteered to go with her, of course, but Susan said she'd only go with Chloe. I think she wanted the chance to talk with her grand-daughter privately.'

217

'You should have insisted on taking Bernard with you and gone as one group,' I said. 'That would have been safest.'

'Would it?' said Stuart. 'Twice now I've led people through the house and both times I lost someone. First the professor and then Marjorie.' He looked at me steadily. 'Did you find her?'

'Yes,' I said. 'She's dead. The professor's dead, too. We can talk about the details later. It's complicated.'

'Everything in this house is,' said Stuart.

Penny came over to join us. 'Bernard's quiet now. Almost asleep. All that exertion wore him out. It's easy to forget how old he is.'

'Susan and Chloe had to go up to the top floor,' I said. 'I think it would be best if all four of us go up to join them and escort them back down.'

Penny was shaking her head before I even finished. 'Bernard is in no condition to go anywhere. He's exhausted. You couldn't get him out of that chair with a crowbar. And anyway, I think you and I should handle this ourselves, Ishmael. Don't you?'

She looked at me meaningfully. Stuart picked up on the look, even though he didn't know what it meant.

'What's going on?' he said immediately. 'What do you know about the situation that I don't?'

'You'll have to excuse us, Colonel,' Penny said firmly. 'Ishmael and I need to talk.'

She grabbed me by the arm and steered me over to the other side of the room. Stuart watched us, but said nothing.

'All the way here,' said Penny, quietly but

fiercely, 'you were worried about the Colonel seeing what you can really do and maybe even figuring out who and what you are. If he's with us when we find the *ka* thief and take it down, he's bound to see something he shouldn't. Either that or the *ka* thief might say something about you . . .'

'It's not always about me,' I said. 'I'm damned if I'll lose anyone else to that monster. Too many people have died already.'

'We can do this,' Penny said forcefully. 'Bernard would only get in the way, and having Stuart around would only complicate things. Stop arguing, Ishmael. You know I'm right.'

I nodded, reluctantly, and looked over at Stuart, who was studying both of us suspiciously.

'You stay here and guard Bernard,' I said. 'We'll find Chloe and Susan, and bring them back down safely.'

Stuart nodded. 'We only have to hang on a little longer. Security should be here soon.'

'Then I'd better get a move on,' I said.

I went hurrying back through the house again, so quickly Penny had to struggle to keep up. I was driven by a terrible feeling of urgency. I had to get to Chloe and Susan before something bad happened.

'There's far too much running through corridors in this case,' Penny growled, already short of breath.

'Susan and Chloe are probably still on the top floor,' I said, 'searching for the cigar case.'

'Three flights of stairs . . .' groaned Penny. 'I swear this case will be the death of me.'

I didn't like the sound of that, so I tried for the light touch again.

'I could always pick you up and carry you,' I said. 'Or sling you over one shoulder in a fireman's lift.'

The look she gave me was full of things best not said aloud.

By the time we reached the first flight of stairs, Penny was struggling to keep up with me, her stamina used up by the day's events. I couldn't slow my pace. The feeling of terrible urgency wouldn't let me.

'Look, go on without me,' Penny said breathlessly. 'I'll catch up.'

I nodded, and broke into a run. I left her without glancing back. Because Penny was vulnerable to the *ka* thief, and I wasn't.

I hit the stairs at a dead run, pounded up them two steps at a time, and just kept going. When I reached the top of the third flight I wasn't even breathing hard, but I could still hear Penny wheezing and gasping down below as she finished the first. I looked at the corridor stretching away before me. Everything seemed quiet enough, but I knew better than to trust appearances in Cardavan House.

I started forward, heading for Bernard and Susan's suite of rooms at the far end, and then I heard a scream. I sprinted down the corridor, covering the ground at inhuman speed, and burst into the suite through the open door. And there was Chloe, with her hands clasped tightly on either side of Susan's head. The *ka* thief had a new body, a new identity to hide behind.

I could see the life energies streaming out of Susan and into Chloe: a rainbow of coruscating lights, vivid and glorious, beautiful beyond bearing. Which made what was happening to them even more horrible. Chloe sucked them in with an endless hunger and an unspeakable delight. The transfer shut off abruptly as the last of Susan's life disappeared into Chloe. She let go of Susan, and the dead body fell limply to the floor. Chloe turned to face me. Her body language had changed completely. She didn't stand like a woman. It was like looking at something wearing a human coat. Her smile was cold and triumphant. And utterly inhuman.

'It doesn't matter what you do, you'll always be too late. Because you are flesh, with flesh's limitations. Humans are such easy prey. And so tasty! Trapped in the dark in that useless body, I had a long time to think about all the things I would do to people once I was free again. I'm going to have so much fun playing with my toys till they break—'

'I won't let that happen,' I said.

'You can't stop me! I could eat up this whole world and still not be satisfied . . .'

'Who are you?' I said. 'What are you?'

'Don't you know? Don't you recognize me, old enemy?'

Chloe cocked her head on one side to see me more clearly. The same way Rose had done.

'Did something happen to you when your ship crashed? Something bad enough to make you forget two species bound together in a glorious history of blood and horror? So . . . you have to come to me for the truth. Of what you are and what you're for . . . How amusing. Very well! Here is wisdom for those who have the strength to stand it. Your kind and mine have been at war for longer than our recorded histories. Generations of us have died with our teeth buried in each other's throats.'

'So you *can* be killed,' I said.

Chloe glared at me for interrupting. 'Everything that lives comes to an end. But however long anyone lives, it's never enough. That's why my ancestors taught themselves how to take lives from the less deserving; it's not like they were doing anything useful with their lives, after all.'

'What's your species called?' I said. 'What's your name?'

'Name?' The thing inside Chloe giggled horribly. 'What do names matter? That's such a transitory notion when you can be as many things as you choose. So many questions! Are you playing for time, old enemy, waiting for reinforcements to arrive? Or your little human pet, perhaps? Oh, I can't wait for her to join us. What would hurt you most, I wonder? Watching me eating her up right in front of you? Or being tortured by the knowledge that I'm living inside her and making her do terrible things, until you're forced to kill her?'

A cold hand clutched at my heart, but I didn't allow anything to show in my face. I couldn't give Chloe, or the thing inside her, even the smallest advantage.

'What happened?' I said. 'What happened between your people and mine to make us hate each other so much?'

Chloe shrugged. 'No one remembers. I think

222

once we found out just how much fun war is we just never wanted it to stop. It's good to have a purpose in life.'

'I don't know you,' I said. 'I don't remember you, or your war.'

'I do,' said Chloe.

'Tell me how you came to be here.'

'Why should I?'

'Because you want to,' I said. 'You love lecturing me and proving your superiority.'

'How right you are!' said Chloe. 'I want you to know everything, just so I can enjoy the look on your face. All those years ago, my ship crashed in what was then Ancient Egypt. Shot down . . .'

'By my people?'

'Oh, get over yourself!' said Chloe. 'You aren't the only ones with good reason to fear my kind. Anyway, the ship and its crew were destroyed by the impact. All that survived was one very special machine. A container for my intelligence, transferred from the original crystal . . .'

'You're crystal creatures?' I said.

'That surprises you? You *have* gone native, haven't you? The local barbarians carried away what they thought was an object of power; a magical jewel. I think they liked the way lights moved within it. It ended up in the hands of Queen Cleopatra. An appalling creature. I liked her immediately. I thought we could be useful to each other, so I made contact with her. She wasn't surprised; her kind talked with gods every day. The idea was that I would teach her people the wonders of science, and then she would have them build me a new ship.

'But instead she just used me to make herself strong, dominate her people and suck the life out of her enemies . . . Just because she could. And she kept on doing it until she'd drained the machine's energies! I was so weakened by the crash I couldn't stop her. I couldn't even recharge the machine in that primitive environment. I was forced to shut it down, go dormant, just to protect myself. I wish I could have seen the look on Cleopatra's face when all her power disappeared in a moment. Her own people dragged her down and took the machine away from her. They executed her while they were sure they could, and then hid the machine inside her mummified body. With a special lock on the sarcophagus lid, just in case.

'The machine took centuries to recharge itself. Until finally I was able to reach out and influence the minds closest to me. The tomb was found and opened, the mummy brought out into the world again. And I arranged for it to be brought to this country.'

'Why?'

'Because I sensed that one of your ships had crashed here not long ago. Do try to keep up!'

'Were you looking for me?' I said. 'Did you want my help to get you off-planet?'

Chloe looked at me as though I was mad or simple. 'No! I just wanted to kill one of you again!'

'But why here? Why Cardavan House?'

Chloe smiled smugly. She was having a good time, forcing me to ask question after question and then teasing me with the smallest possible pieces of information.

'I have always been well served by the weaknesses of others. I needed someone who would guard and protect me. And who better than some poor fool who thought I belonged to him?'

'So,' I said, 'basically you're an alien AI of sorts, a crystal intelligence in a piece of alien tech. Moving from one human hiding place to another, so you can kill undetected.'

'That is such limited human thinking,' said Chloe. 'How have you fallen so far? How do you stand it?'

'Why did you start killing people here?' I said doggedly. 'Why reveal yourself?'

'Because of you, of course! The moment you arrived, old enemy, it set off all kinds of alarms in my head . . . But I couldn't find you, you'd disguised yourself so well. Still, I knew if I just kept feeding I'd eventually get to you.'

'But when you tried to take my life energies, you couldn't,' I said. 'What happened? Performance anxiety?'

Chloe scowled at me. 'You've done something to yourself. You're not what I expected. But it doesn't matter. I'll just eat up everyone else here until I'm strong enough to batter my way through these new defences of yours. Another victory in the war that never ends! Another chance for my kind to revenge themselves on yours.'

'I don't remember you,' I said. 'There's no quarrel between us. We don't have to be enemies.'

'Of course we do!' said Chloe. 'Your very existence offends me. The war will never end until every one of your kind has been wiped from the universe.'

225

'And then?' I said.

'What?'

'What will you do then? When all of my kind are gone?'

Chloe shrugged. 'I don't know. Find someone else to hate, I suppose.'

'There has to be something better you could be doing with your lives.'

'There is nothing better!' And then Chloe stopped, looking slyly at the open doorway. 'She's almost here. Your little favourite. I know I've only just eaten, but there's always room for dessert.'

'Don't come in, Penny!' I said loudly. 'It's in here! It'll kill you!'

But the footsteps out in the corridor didn't even slow. Penny appeared in the doorway, her breathing back under control again, ready for anything. And then she saw Susan lying dead on the floor, with Chloe standing over her, smiling her cold inhuman smile.

'Oh, shit!' said Penny.

'Yes!' I said. 'Get out of here, Penny, please. Let me handle this.'

'We're partners,' said Penny. 'We work best together. You need me to keep you human.'

'That isn't going to help this time,' I said. 'Go, Penny!'

'Too late!' Chloe said happily.

She threw herself at Penny, her clawed hands reaching out eagerly. I threw myself between them and grabbed hold of Chloe's wrists, just as I had with Professor Rose. Chloe fought me with the same inhuman strength and we staggered back and forth across the room, knocking over furniture and smashing delicate irreplaceable ornaments. The thing inside her laughed happily. Fighting not just to hurt me, but to get past me to get to Penny. Burning up Chloe's life energies to do it, because it didn't care what it did to its host.

I tried to restrain Chloe without hurting her, but the alien within her made that impossible. And in the end Chloe jerked her wrists out of my hands, because the only way I could have held on to her would have been to break them. I held my ground, standing between her and Penny. Chloe lashed out with her small bony fists, hitting me again and again. All I could do was keep my arms up and endure the punishment. I didn't cry out. I wouldn't give her the satisfaction. And then Chloe stopped fighting, and smiled at something behind me.

'Well! Look who's here!'

I felt my blood run cold as I heard Stuart's voice.

'Ishmael! What are you doing!'

Chloe grinned at me triumphantly. I grabbed hold of her while she was distracted, spun her round and held her tightly from behind, pinning her arms to her side. She fought me savagely, but her new unnatural strength was no use against the leverage I had.

'Let her go!' said Stuart. He stood in the doorway beside Penny, glaring at me. 'Stop that! You're hurting her!'

'Help me, Stuart!' said Chloe. She sounded perfectly normal, and the face she showed Stuart looked just like his wife's. 'Ishmael's gone mad! He's the killer! Kill him, before he kills me!'

Stuart produced a gun from inside his jacket. The gun he swore he hadn't brought with him. I should have known: a soldier never goes unarmed. He aimed his gun at me, and Chloe stopped struggling to give him a clearer shot at me. Penny grabbed Stuart's arm and tried to wrestle the gun away from him. He threw her to one side with casual strength, not taking his eyes off me for a moment. Penny hit the floor hard and didn't move. Stuart aimed the gun at my face. His hand was very steady.

'Kill him, Stuart!' said Chloe.

She sounded less like the real thing now, but I wasn't sure Stuart had noticed. I stood very still.

'Look at her,' I said, keeping my voice calm and reasonable. 'Listen to her. This isn't your Chloe. She's been possessed by an alien intelligence. That's what's been happening here. Look what she did to Susan.'

Stuart looked at the body on the floor, and a slow uncertainty appeared in his face. He had heard of such things. He looked carefully at Chloe, and didn't like something he saw in her face. He didn't lower his gun, but for the first time he didn't seem so sure about what he should do. Chloe screamed and swore at him, pleading and insulting, trying everything to get him to shoot me. But the louder she screamed, the less she sounded like Chloe. And then, quite suddenly, she stopped trying. She stood very still and laughed at Stuart. A nasty, mocking sound. He flinched at the sound of

228

it. The gun moved to target Chloe, and she laughed even harder.

'You don't have to shoot her!' I said quickly. 'Just help me subdue her, until we can figure out some way to get the alien out of her.'

'I'll never let that happen!' Chloe said viciously.

Stuart looked at Susan, unmoving on the floor.

'Yes!' said Chloe. 'I killed her! I killed all of them! And I'll keep doing it till every single one of you is dead!'

Stuart looked at her steadily, his gun aimed at her face. 'I don't know if you can hear me in there, Chloe, but I can't let that happen. I have to stop this, now. I'm so sorry . . .'

His finger tightened on the trigger. I didn't know what to do: killing Chloe might kill the alien or just release it. But then Stuart's hand trembled and he lowered the gun until it was pointing at the floor. And while I was watching what Stuart was doing, Chloe back-elbowed me in the ribs, knocking the breath out of me. I couldn't hold on to her any more. She broke away from me, and ran straight past Stuart and out of the room. He didn't even try to stop her. I could hear her laughing happily as she ran down the corridor. Penny rose painfully slowly to her feet, to stand beside Stuart. He looked at her and then at me. His face was full of misery.

'I couldn't do it,' he said.

'Of course you couldn't,' I said.

Nine
The Jewel in the Mummy

Stuart pulled his military dignity around him like the uniform he used to wear. And just like that, he was himself again. His back straightened, his mouth firmed, and his usual calm authority settled back in place. He nodded to me, and I nodded back.

And then I looked at the gun he was holding. 'You said you hadn't brought a weapon?'

He looked at the gun with a 'This old thing?' expression and put it away inside his jacket. Which had to have been expertly and expensively tailored to hide a bulge like that. He smiled briefly.

'I didn't want the family to worry,' he said. 'It wouldn't have fitted the image they had of me as just a civil servant.' He looked at the open doorway. 'Chloe's still out there. We have to go after her.'

He was saying all the right things, everything he thought he was supposed to say, but he couldn't put any emotion into it. He knew his duty, knew what he had to do. He just didn't know how to do it.

'There's no hurry,' I said. 'After all, where can she go? The house is still locked up. She can't leave until Security get here, and they'll probably have to break in. How long before that happens?'

'God knows!' said Stuart. 'They should have been here by now.'

'We'll find her,' I said.

'Can I just point out that we don't know who locked the doors?' said Penny.

'Of course you can,' I said. 'And I will point out in return that it doesn't really matter. The alien doesn't want to leave. It doesn't want us to leave. It wants all of us dead, so there's no one left to raise the alarm and warn the world.'

'Tell me about this alien,' said Stuart. 'I want to know everything. Right now. And I don't give a damn how complicated it is.'

'Understandable,' I said. 'But first, where's Bernard?'

Penny made a startled noise and glared at Stuart. 'I only just realized he isn't here! Tell me you didn't leave him down there on his own!'

Stuart cleared his throat, but didn't look guilty. The Colonel didn't really do guilty. 'I found it necessary to leave the drawing room for a while. Bernard had fallen asleep in his chair and was snoring. Quite remarkably loudly. So I went out into the corridor for a little peace and quiet. And then . . . I thought I heard Chloe calling out to me from upstairs. As though she was in danger. I knew I shouldn't leave Bernard unguarded, but it sounded like Chloe needed me more. So I made sure the drawing room door was properly closed and headed for the stairs.'

He sounded perfectly calm and reasonable. As though he'd only done what could be

231

expected under the circumstances. But he was having a hard time meeting my eyes. He'd left a tired out old man he was supposed to be protecting all on his own, in a house like a war zone. But then I'd always known that in any situation the Colonel would protect his wife first.

After all, protecting Chloe was why he'd asked me to come to Cardavan House.

'I heard sounds of fighting and followed them here,' said Stuart. He looked steadily at Penny. 'I shouldn't have hit you. I'm sorry.'

'That's all right,' said Penny. 'You were under a lot of stress. But if you ever try that again I will knee you in the balls so hard they'll go back up the way they came down and you'll never see them again.'

I nodded solemnly. 'She would, too.'

'I believe you,' said Stuart.

'All right,' said Penny. 'Let's get back downstairs. Bernard's not safe while Chloe's still running around loose.'

I thought I saw Stuart wince, just for a moment, though whether in respect to Bernard's situation or Chloe's I wasn't sure.

'Do we tell Bernard what's happened to Chloe?' I said. 'And that Susan is dead?'

'No,' said Stuart. 'He wouldn't understand about Chloe, and I don't know how he'd cope with Susan's death. He might launch into one of his rages and attack us, and we might have to hurt him in order to subdue him. And anyway . . . he'd probably just forget and have to be told again and again. Why be cruel? We'll just tell

232

him Susan is still up here, looking for his cigar case.'

He stopped and looked at Susan lying dead on the floor. She seemed such a small thing, in death. But then that's true of most of us.

'Bernard is better off not knowing,' said Stuart. 'Once Security get here, a doctor can give the old man something to keep him calm and we'll get him out of here. It's a shame, but without Susan to look after him I don't see Bernard ever coming back. Even though he and Chloe are all that's left of the Cardavans. And Chloe is . . .'

He couldn't bring himself to finish the thought. Military discipline could only carry him so far.

'We'll find some way to save Chloe from what's inside her,' I said.

He looked at me. 'Do you have any idea how?'

'Not at the moment,' I said. 'But I'm working on it.'

I led the way down the landing, towards the stairs. Taking my time, so I could bring Stuart up to date on what had been happening. Fortunately, years of weird missions had taught me how to be succinct. Penny chimed in now and again, to make sure I didn't miss out on the human angle. She saw that as part of her job, in our partnership. I never told her I sometimes deliberately left things out so she'd feel she was needed. It's all part of being in a relationship. And part of being human, as I understand it. I told Stuart everything he needed to know about the alien, except for the bits that touched on me. Though I still wasn't sure how much of that

I believed. The alien hadn't struck me as being a particularly trustworthy narrator.

I kept a careful lookout as we walked, but there wasn't any sight or a sound of Chloe anywhere. Presumably she'd gone back down into the house, to feed on the only other potential victim left. I didn't mention it out loud, but it had occurred to me that it might be a good idea to leave Bernard on his own as bait in a trap. We could hide and watch, and when Chloe came for Bernard we could all jump her from ambush. I was almost positive we could stop Chloe before Bernard came to any harm. But it still sounded like a plan that needed a lot more thought before it could be presented to Penny and Stuart. So I didn't say anything.

And then I stopped suddenly, as I heard footsteps coming up the stairs. Stuart and Penny stopped with me. I gestured for them to listen, and first Stuart and then Penny nodded quickly, to show they heard the footsteps too. We stood listening as the footsteps drew steadily closer.

'That can't be Chloe,' murmured Penny.

'Doesn't sound like her,' I said.

'And anyway, why would she want to come back?' said Penny. 'She knows she can't take us while we're together.'

'Unless she's killed Bernard for more strength,' said Stuart. 'And we're the only ones left . . .'

He drew his gun and covered the end of the corridor. We stood close together, watching the top of the stairs. Waiting . . . And then Bernard came stomping up into view, red-faced and puffing from the exertion of his climb. Stuart quickly made his gun disappear. Bernard saw us waiting, waved cheerfully, and ambled down the corridor to join us. I did wonder for a moment whether the alien might have transferred itself into Bernard to catch us by surprise. But it seemed unlikely. Why swap a perfectly sound young body for an older and damaged one, just for a moment's advantage? Bernard finally came to a halt before us, and looked reproachfully at Stuart.

'I woke up on my own! You'd all gone off and left me . . . Took me a while to remember where everyone was, until I searched for my cigar case and found I didn't have it. The old memory isn't what it was . . . It felt a bit spooky down there on my own, so I thought I'd come up and help Susan look.'

'She's still in your room,' I said. 'She hasn't found it yet.'

'She'll never find it without me,' said Bernard. 'Even I don't remember where I leave things half the time!'

He seemed remarkably calm and composed after his little rest. Back in control of himself, with no memory at all of his earlier rage.

'Susan said she was going to get changed,' said Penny. 'I don't think she wants to be interrupted. Come back downstairs with us. She'll join us later.'

'Fair enough,' said Bernard.

He extended a gentlemanly arm to Penny. She smiled and slipped her arm through his, and the two of them strolled back to the stairs, chatting companionably together. Once again, a female voice was doing wonders to keep Bernard calm and focused. Stuart and I followed at a distance so we could talk.

'Until we have some idea how to get the alien out of Chloe safely,' said Stuart, 'you are not to do anything that might hurt her.'

'I know,' I said. 'I am working on an idea.'

'Is it a good idea?'

'It's an idea.'

'Try me,' said Stuart.

'I think it all comes back to the jewel in the mummy, the original container and protector of the alien intelligence. The alien had to store its consciousness in the jewel to survive the starship crash, and it's been in there for centuries. I think the jewel makes it possible for the alien's consciousness to jump from body to body, but the alien itself remains inside the jewel. So, if we destroy the jewel . . . we destroy the alien.'

'Nice theory,' said Stuart. 'Elegant, even. And simple. I like simple when there's violence to be done. Do you really think it'll work?'

'It's worth a try,' I said. 'The good thing about my theory is that if I'm right the alien's consciousness can be destroyed but the host body, Chloe, will be left undamaged. In her own right mind again.'

'I love this theory,' said Stuart. 'You know I've always admired your logic, Ishmael.'

'No, stop . . . wait a minute,' I said. 'I'm missing something . . .'

I crashed to a halt and looked quickly around me. Stuart stopped with me, and called out to Penny and Bernard to wait where they were. They

236

stopped and looked back. Penny glared up and down the corridor to make sure we were in no danger. Bernard didn't seem too bothered about anything, as long as he had a pretty girl on his arm. They all watched closely as I strode up and down the corridor, trying to look at everything at once in the hope something would jar loose whatever it was I was trying to remember. It was important, it meant something, and it was right on the tip of my mind . . .

And then I stopped abruptly before one particular door. 'This door was locked the first time Penny and I came up here,' I said. 'I had to break it down to check out the room. It was the only door up here that was locked.'

'Professor Rose's room,' said Penny.

'Of course,' I said. 'The man who took the jewel from the mummy. He kept this door locked because he'd hidden something important in here that he couldn't risk anyone finding.'

'But we searched that room!' said Penny.

'Not thoroughly,' I said. 'We didn't know what we were looking for then.'

The door flew open. And there was Chloe standing in the doorway, blocking the way. Still smiling her horrible smile. 'I heard you! You can't have the jewel, it's mine!'

'You mean it's you,' I said.

'Who is that?' Bernard asked querulously. He sounded more frightened than confused. 'That thing . . . it looks like Chloe, but it isn't her. What is it?'

Chloe turned her smile on him and he flinched. Her smile widened. 'Out of the mouths of the mentally impoverished . . . No, Bernard, I'm not your little Chloe. I'm the big bad wolf and I've eaten her all up. I'm also the reason why your precious Susan isn't around any more . . .'

'Susan?' said Bernard. 'I don't understand. Susan is in our rooms.'

'Well, yes and no,' said Chloe. She scowled, as she realized Bernard didn't understand. 'Susan's dead! I killed her! And now you're all on your own . . . How ever will you cope?'

The alien couldn't resist a chance to be cruel, but shouldn't have taunted him. Bernard roared with rage and charged straight at Chloe. He hit her straight on and drove her back into Rose's room. Chloe clamped both her hands on to Bernard's head and they stumbled to a halt. I was already charging into the room after them, afraid I'd lost another victim to the alien, but Chloe snatched her hands away from Bernard and looked at him in disgust.

'You're no use to me! You're too damaged!'

Bernard snapped out of his daze. He drew back his fist, and Chloe hit him with a vicious back sweep of her arm. The impact picked him up and threw him across the room. He slammed into the far wall with terrible force and slid down the wall to sit slumped on the floor, his head hanging forward limply. I couldn't tell whether he was still breathing. Chloe spun round to face me, her smile back in place. Stuart moved in beside me and pointed his gun at her. She laughed in his face.

'You know you can't do it.'

Stuart pulled the trigger. The bullet narrowly

238

missed Chloe's head. She looked at him incredulously, then darted to one side. Stuart opened fire
again, and again the bullet only just missed her.
He kept firing as she dodged back and forth, and
I realized Stuart was deliberately missing every
time. He was intent on shaking the alien's confi-
dence and holding its attention, to give me time
to come up with something. And then Stuart ran
out of bullets. He lowered his gun and set about
reloading, calmly and methodically.

'Find the jewel, Ishmael,' he said quietly.
'Penny, your turn to keep the alien occupied. I'll
do what I can, but these are all the bullets I've
got left.'

Penny picked up a handy crystal ornament and
threw it at Chloe, who ducked it easily. She
grabbed up one thing after another and threw them
all at Chloe, and as she pressed forward Chloe
backed away. Penny shot me a 'Get on with it!'
look. I knew she couldn't hold Chloe off for long,
but I let her do it because she made the best bait.
Chloe wanted Penny. I eased past both of them
to take up a position in the middle of the room.
The jewel had to be here somewhere.

Chloe tried to grab hold of Penny, to pull her
close. Penny dodged away and kept throwing
things. Chloe turned on me. Stuart sent a bullet
right past her face. Chloe fell back, and Penny
kicked her in the arse. The alien spun round to
face her again.

I looked steadily around the room, not allowing
myself to be distracted by what was happening.
The jewel had to be here, or Chloe wouldn't have
holed up in this room to guard it.

Penny grabbed a blanket off the bed and threw it over Chloe's head. And while the alien was temporarily blinded, Penny picked up a wooden chair and hit Chloe over the head with it. The chair didn't break and Chloe didn't go down. She threw the blanket off and Penny backed away, holding the chair out before her.

'That always works in the movies . . . Are you getting anywhere yet, Ishmael? Only I'm slowing down and she isn't!'

Chloe's face was flushed an unhealthy colour, and she was breathing hard. The alien was burning up Chloe's life energies to gain speed and strength, and didn't care what damage that did to the host body. After all, the alien expected to have Penny's body soon. I had to find the jewel before it was too late to save either of them. How was I supposed to find the damned thing? It wasn't like it left a trail of scent, like Marjorie . . .

And then I remembered . . . The jewel had been hidden inside the mummy's chest for centuries, sealed up inside the sarcophagus. So it must have picked up the same rich spicy scent as the mummy. Not enough for human senses to detect. But up here, away from the collection, it might be discernible to me . . . I breathed in deeply, turning my head slowly back and forth. Ignoring the growing commotion behind me. Until I picked up traces of the mummy's scent, coming from inside the wardrobe before me.

I ran over to it and yanked the door open, and there were the four identical suits I'd seen earlier. I searched quickly through the pockets, and found the jewel in the inside pocket of the second jacket. I took it out. The jewel was a nasty purplish crimson colour, like blood that had gone off. Shimmering lights flickered deep inside it. I turned round and held the jewel up so everyone could see it. All motion in the room came to an abrupt halt.

Chloe stared at the jewel. She took a step forward, almost in spite of herself, and then stopped. 'You can't have that. It's mine.'

I nodded to Penny, and she backed quickly away from the alien to stand with Stuart. He still had his gun aimed at Chloe.

'It doesn't have to end here,' I said, to the alien inside Chloe. 'No one else has to die. Get out of Chloe and put yourself back in the jewel. You'll be safe there. And maybe in the future someone will find a way to get you home.'

'Place myself in the hands of my enemies? Never!'

'Be reasonable,' I said.

'Never!'

I hefted the jewel in my hand and looked to Stuart. 'Care to do the honours, Colonel?'

'Love to,' said Stuart.

Chloe surged forward, grabbing for the jewel. I tossed it lightly up into the air. Stuart fired once, and the jewel exploded into a thousand pieces. Chloe screamed briefly and then collapsed, crumpling bonelessly to the floor. But I could still hear the alien screaming, its horrid voice slowly disappearing in a direction I could sense but not name . . . Until it faded away and was gone.

Stuart put his gun away and hurried forward. He sat down with Chloe, lifted her up and cradled her in his arms. She stirred slowly, her eyes flickering.

'Nice shooting, Colonel,' I said.

'It's all in the training,' he said.

'Did it bother you that I was so close to the jewel?'

'No,' he said, not taking his eyes off Chloe. 'It didn't bother me at all.'

Penny came over to join me, and we leaned on each other tiredly. We'd both been running on adrenalin so long that we had nothing but fumes left to keep us going.

'At least it's over now,' said Penny.

'Is it?' I said.

Penny looked into my face and pushed herself away from me. 'You had to spoil the moment . . . What is it, Ishmael?'

'I'm not sure,' I said. 'It's just that . . . the alien always killed its victims the same way. By sucking the life energies out of them. But George was beaten to death. I can't help thinking that means something.'

Stuart helped Chloe to her feet. She shook her head slowly and grimaced.

'Are you all right?' said Stuart. 'How do you feel?'

'Awful,' said Chloe. Her voice sounded strained, from all the shouting someone else had done using her vocal chords. 'I've got a head like you wouldn't believe, and every muscle I've got is aching like I just ran a marathon . . . What happened? How did I end up here?'

Stuart looked at me suddenly. 'Can we be sure—'

I knew what he was asking, and quickly shook my head. 'Don't worry, that's Chloe. I'd know if it wasn't, now I know what to look for. And you'd know, anyway.'

'Yes,' said Stuart. 'I would.'

We both asked Chloe a few tactful questions, but it was clear she had no memory of anything she'd done while the alien was in control. Which was probably just as well.

'Take her downstairs, Stuart,' I said. 'You could probably both use something bracing to drink . . .'

Chloe looked at Bernard, sitting slumped by the wall with his head hanging down. 'He's dead, isn't he?'

'Penny and I will take care of everything,' I said.

Stuart led Chloe out of the room. I could hear her bombarding him with questions, all the way down the corridor. Penny looked at me.

'You've got that look on your face. You've worked something out, haven't you? What?'

'All along I said the manner of George's death spoke to rage as a motive. What person in this house has always had the most of that?'

We both turned to look at Bernard. His head slowly came up and his eyes opened. He smiled, briefly.

'Took you long enough.'

I knelt down before him, so we could look each other in the face. Penny crouched down beside

243

me. Bernard's eyes moved from me to her and back again, but otherwise he didn't move. His face was drawn and ashen, but his gaze was surprisingly clear and focused. I checked his pulse, then looked at Penny and shook my head slightly. Bernard managed a small chuckle.

'No need for diplomacy, boy. I'm dying. I can feel it. Something important broke when I hit the wall. And yet . . . I'm thinking more clearly now than I've been able to in some time. Nothing like imminent death to concentrate the mind . . . Or maybe a candle always burns brightest just before it goes out. Susan's dead, isn't she?'

'Yes,' said Penny. 'I'm so sorry.'

'And the thing that got inside Chloe?' said Bernard.

'Dead and gone,' I said.

'Good,' said Bernard. 'That's good. There really was an ancient curse after all, and we brought it on ourselves.'

'You killed George?' I said.

'Yes. Yes, I did.'

'You were the only one he would have let back into that room while he was gloating over his mummy, so he could rub your nose in it one more time. You were the only one who could have been so angry with him and had the strength to bludgeon him to death like that. And then you used your own keys to lock the door after you. Did Susan cover for you while you changed out of your blood-soaked clothes?'

'Yes. It's a terrible thing to say, but neither of us ever really cared much for George. He was a trial as a child, and a bully as an adult.'

'You should rest,' said Penny. 'Save your strength. Security will be here soon. We'll get you a doctor . . .'

'There's nothing anyone can do for me now,' said Bernard. 'And nothing I'd want them to do. I killed my son.'

'Why?' said Penny.

'Because he was an ungrateful little shit who took everything away from me,' Bernard said flatly. 'Including my own home. Everyone in this family has cared for the collection, but he obsessed over it. The damn fool embezzled money from his own business to pay for that mummy. I only found out by accident while I was searching his study. Marjorie had been dropping increasingly heavy hints about changes in George's will . . . and I was looking for proof. Instead, I discovered George had left a hole in the family business accounts so big you could drive a tank through it. God knows how he planned to make it good again.'

I just nodded. I finally understood why Stuart had asked me to come to Cardavan House. But it didn't matter after all.

'But why kill George?' said Penny.

'I didn't mean to,' said Bernard. 'I'm sure I didn't. We argued, right there in front of the mummy in its coffin. I told him I knew about all the money he'd stolen. That he'd have to sell the mummy, or half the collection, to cover his debts. He laughed at me. Told me he'd never get rid of any of it. That the collection had always been more important than the family. He shouldn't have laughed at me. I stormed out of the room, shaking

245

all over. I was so angry . . . I just snatched up the nearest heavy object to hand, then strode back in and struck him down. I'm sure I only meant to hurt him, the way he'd hurt me. But once I started hitting him I couldn't stop. I didn't want to. It only ended when I was too tired to hit him any more. I never knew I had so much anger in me.

'Fortunately, I'd had enough sense to shut down the house's security cameras before I went to the room where the mummy was. So no one would have to know what George had done to the family finances. I still had all the passwords because George never got around to changing them. When I went upstairs to change my clothes I kept expecting to bump into someone, and then I'd have had to explain what I'd done. But I never met anyone. I just . . . got away with it. And afterwards I forgot I'd ever done it. I'd forgotten so many things . . . but I think this time I wanted to forget.'

'You locked the front and back doors, didn't you?' I said. 'You still had a complete set of keys from when this was your own home.'

'I didn't want anyone leaving,' said Bernard. 'By that point I wasn't sure why, I just knew something wasn't right. It never occurred to me that the killer I didn't want to escape was myself.'

'No one else has to know,' I said. 'Chloe doesn't need to know.'

Bernard managed another small smile. 'Thank you for that. You know . . . dying is easy. It's Alzheimer's that's hard.'

And then he just stopped breathing.

Ten
Afterwards

We stood together outside the front door of Cardavan House, waiting for the security people to show up. Penny and me, Stuart and Chloe. I found Bernard's set of keys in one of his pockets. We all felt the need to step outside the house, to get some fresh air and put a little distance between ourselves and everything that had happened. A cold wind blew across the open ground, and the dark starry skies were still some time short of morning.

We filled Chloe in on most of what had been happening, and why. She took it in her stride, because working for Black Heir does that to you.

I didn't say anything about Bernard's confession. In my report, the alien could take the blame for all the deaths. So Chloe could remember her grandfather the way he used to be.

'I was in the field all along, taking on an invading alien, and never knew it,' Chloe said finally. 'Not exactly the experience I thought it would be! How do you people manage? How do you cope with all the . . . madness?'

'If you even start to say it's all in the training, I will hit you . . .' Penny said to me.

'All right, I won't say it,' I said. 'But I am thinking it very loudly.'

Chloe looked at Stuart. 'I still don't know who you really work for. And you're not going to tell me, are you?'

'Work hard for Black Heir for another twenty years,' said Stuart, 'and you might have a security clearance high enough to find out for yourself.'

'You know you're going to tell me eventually . . .'

'Possibly. But eventually isn't now. Do you remember anything from when you were under the alien's control?'

Chloe frowned, and her hands twisted together. 'Not really. Just . . . moments, like dreams. It seems to me that I called out to you for help. And you heard me, and came to save me.'

'Of course,' said Stuart. 'I'll always hear you, wherever you are.'

'And now . . . I'm the last of the Cardavans,' said Chloe. 'No one else left. Apart from a few distant cousins.'

'You still have me,' said Stuart.

'And the house,' I said.

Everyone looked at me.

'What?' said Chloe.

'Well, with Marjorie gone, everything will revert to the family,' I said. 'Which means you get everything. The house, the collection, the mummy . . .'

I stopped and looked at Penny. 'Why did you just elbow me in the ribs, really hard?'

'Little Mister Tact,' said Penny.

'I don't want any of it,' Chloe said firmly. 'That damned collection has dominated my family for far too long. You'll help me get rid of it all, won't you, Stuart?'

'I can do that,' said Stuart. 'I know some people . . .'

'For a really good price, of course.'

'Of course, dear,' said Stuart. He looked at me. 'What are we going to tell the security people, when they finally arrive? Don't think I won't be having some very harsh words with whoever's in charge! Even allowing for how far we are from everywhere, a response time like this is utterly unacceptable.'

'We'll tell them Professor Rose killed everyone,' I said. 'Dropping everything on the dry old stick is a bit hard on him, but you said Rose had no family. So we'll say he became obsessed with the Cardavan collection and the mummy in particular, and wanted it for himself. He killed George because George denied him access to the collection after they quarrelled one time too many. Then he stole the mummy and hid it. And used some rare Egyptian poison to kill all the others, because he was afraid he'd be found out. Something exotic that he picked up on his travels.'

'A good enough story for public consumption,' said Stuart. 'With the gem gone, there's no proof the alien was ever here.' He turned to Chloe. 'And we don't need to bother Black Heir about any of this, dear. You know what they're like. You could end up in one of their secret laboratories, while they dig through your mind searching for anything the alien might have left behind.'

'You're right, as always,' said Chloe. 'They can keep their field work! I never want to get this close to an alien ever again.'

'Very wise,' said Stuart.

Chloe suddenly shuddered. 'I'm cold. I think I'll go back inside. I feel in need of a drink. In fact, I feel in need of several large drinks followed by very large chasers, all in the same glass. With an olive. Would anyone else care to join me?'

I gave the nod to Penny and she smiled brightly at Chloe before accompanying her indoors, so Stuart and I could have some time together. The door shut behind them, and I nodded to Stuart.

'Case over, Colonel,' I said. 'All the mysteries solved.'

'The Organization will require a full report on everything that happened here.'

'I'll see they get one.'

'Thank you,' said Stuart, 'for saving Chloe.'

'That's why you brought me here,' I said. 'I only wish I could have saved the others.'

'You can only follow where the case leads,' said Stuart. 'Now you and Penny should leave before Security arrive. They're a bit too public for you.'

'Of course,' I said.

'I'll take care of the clean-up,' said Stuart. 'Make sure everyone understands the official version of events, and see that all the bodies are properly put to rest. That's my department.'

'Too many people died,' I said, 'before I was able to solve the case. And this isn't the first time that's happened. If I'm going to be sent out on more of these murder mysteries, I need to do better. I would appreciate any help or advice you can offer me, Colonel.'

'Of course,' he said.

We shared a brief smile. Two professionals who understood each other.

'You know,' said Stuart, 'I do have some questions as to how you were able to . . .'

I looked at him and he looked at me, and we both smiled again.

'Tell me,' said Stuart, 'do you know why so many alien starships end up crashing on our world?'

'I think so,' I said. 'It's because bigger countries have always preferred to fight their wars in other people's countries.'

Stuart looked up at the night sky, full of stars that shone so brightly from so far away.

'We have no idea at all of what's really going on out there, do we?'

'No,' I said truthfully. 'We don't.'